the Pretty One

SELECTED BOOKS BY JAN YAGER
[a/k/a J.L. (Janet) Barkas]

NOVELS AND POETRY

Untimely Death
(with Fred Yager)
Just Your Everyday People
(with Fred Yager)
The Healing Power of Creative Mourning: Poems
(with Fred Yager, Priscilla Orr, Seth Alan Barkas, and Scott Yager)

NONFICTION BOOKS

When Friendship Hurts
Friendshifts®
Victims
365 Daily Affirmations for Creative Weight Management
Who's That Sitting at My Desk?
Work Less, Do More
Creative Time Management for the New Millennium
Creative Time Management
125 Ways to Meet the Love of Your Life
Single in America
The Help Book
Road Signs on Life's Journey
Effective Business & Nonfiction Writing
Business Protocol
Making Your Office Work for You
Career Opportunities in the Film Industry
(with Fred Yager)
Career Opportunities in the Publishing Industry
(with Fred Yager)
Friendship: A Selected, Annotated Bibliography
Meatless Cooking: Celebrity Style
The Vegetable Passion: A History of the Vegetarian State of Mind

the Pretty One

A Novel

Jan Yager

HANNACROIX CREEK BOOKS, INC.
Stamford, Connecticut

For my family and friends

Interior Layout & Design by Scribe Freelance | www.scribefreelance.com

Library of Congress Cataloging-in-Publication Data

Yager, Jan, 1948-
  The pretty one : a novel / Jan Yager.
      p. cm.
  ISBN 978-1-889262-71-0 (hardcover)—ISBN 978-1-889262-70-3 (trade pbk.)
  1. Women psychologists--Fiction. 2. Success--Fiction. 3. Compulsive eating--Fiction. 4. Abusive parents--Fiction. 5. Adult child sexual abuse victims--Fiction. 6. Mothers and daughters--Fiction. I. Title.
  PS3625.A36P74 2011
  813'.6--dc22

                          2010024027

PRAISE FOR
THE PRETTY ONE BY JAN YAGER

———

"Bravely takes you to the heart and hell of a compulsive over-eater yet offers hope for healing too."

—Dr. Cynthia Allison, psychologist

"*The Pretty One* is a dramatic and moving account of the profound impact of body image on women's lives. This book will assist others in examining and healing the emotional wounds that are currently being filled with food."

—Christine A. Hartline, MA, Executive Director,
Eating Disorder Referral and Information Center
http://www.edreferral.com

"In *The Pretty One*, Jan Yager captures the emotional ups and downs that accompany the main character's battles with her weight. Emily's story is told in a unique style that mixes flash-backs with real time narration and brings up causes for her food problems."

—Leigh Cohn, Editor-in-Chief, *Eating Disorders:
The Journal of Treatment and Prevention*

"In *The Pretty One*, Jan Yager broaches all the very difficult subjects that a lot of people don't want to look at but must, if they want to overcome them in their own lives."

—Suzanne Vaughan, *Potholes & Parachutes*

Part One
The Limelight

THE CAR ARRIVED right on time—but that didn't stop Emily Taylor from worrying. But then, Emily worried about everything. She worried about whether she had done the right thing by accepting the producer's offer to send a car to drive her from her suburban New Jersey home to the television studio in Manhattan. Would the producer hold it against her? As far as Emily was concerned, driving herself was not even an option. That would make her even more anxious. What if she had an accident because she was distracted, going over in her mind what she should say, or if she'd made the right decision about what she was wearing? She couldn't ask her husband, Greg, to drive her. He had to stay at home to get their kids off to school. Should she have allowed the boys to miss one day so they could all drive in to Manhattan together? But then the boys and Greg would have to go with her to the studio, and that might look unprofessional. Plus, she didn't want her sons to miss a day of school on her account.

She could have stayed at a hotel near the studio but she hated to be away from Greg for even one night. Besides, it would be harder to get ready for the show the next morning from a hotel room. She was still debating what outfit to wear when she concluded that accepting the offer to have a car drive her round trip was the best solution.

That put aside, she moved on to other worries. Had she studied her answers to the questions enough? Or had she analyzed them too much so she risked sounding forced and stale? Would the interviewer stick to the questions that she and the producer had gone over? Or would the hostess ad lib, as she was known to do?

As a clinical psychologist, Emily would diagnose such constant worry in one of her clients as generalized anxiety disorder. And treat it by urging the client to talk about her feelings, and so explore why her notions of what others thought about her resulted in such anxiety. Was it a *hunger* for acceptance that caused her to worry so much? Emily would ask. And did she self-medicate with food to soothe the anxiety or the rage that burned beneath emotional wounds that wouldn't heal?—Stop with the self-diagnosis, Emily chided herself. What was it Greg always said? "You can't see the forest if you're a tree."

Hunger was Emily's friend as well as her demon. It lay at the core of her life-long struggle with over-eating and obesity. It was a battle she had won and lost many times over the past 25 years, and this morning she was on the winning side, having recently shed 60 pounds to be back to her wedding weight of 135.

Emily entered the bathroom one last time to check her hair in case there were no stylists on hand at the studio. She peered into the mirror and scrutinized her bangs, which she'd styled to cover up a two-inch scar on her forehead that she got when she was an infant. She'd been covering that scar most of her life and she sure didn't want to reveal it to five million television viewers now.

So many questions ran through Emily's mind as she did another check of her attaché case and pocketbook for everything she might possibly need: lipstick (no, she didn't really need that since the station would make her up by a professional make-up artist, but it was still better to have her own bright red lipstick "just in case"); a mirror for last-minute fussing in the car; a copy of her book, of course, maybe even two or three copies in case they didn't have one or she met someone that she wanted to give it to; a hair brush (she really preferred that they use hers when they made her up and did her hair since she distrusted that their brushes were really sterilized for each guest); and money. She wanted at least sixty dollars in her wallet, including a $50 bill hidden under her driver's license, and various bank cards on the left side so she wouldn't feel poor (it was important to feel successful and not intimidated by this experience). She also had her cell phone, the lifeline between Greg and her throughout the hours ahead; a pen, pencil, and business cards, in case someone wanted to get in contact with her afterwards.

This television appearance was something she had been

preparing for ever since she had been a guest on that same show twenty-five years ago. That was half her lifetime, when she was just twenty-five. Back then it was much more unusual for a relatively unknown psychologist and book author to be a guest on a major morning talk show. In those days they only booked best-selling authors or world-famous psychologists. It was hard for Emily to believe that it really had been twenty-five years since she was on this show. Emily had accomplished a great deal in the ensuing years—but nothing that warranted another appearance on a national television show until now.

Looking back, she had been precocious and an overachiever when she was twenty-five. Yes, she had accomplished so much, so young, but she was much more focused then. It was easier to accomplish something when she sacrificed her every moment to her career. While other women her age pursued husbands and babies, Emily worked night and day, writing her first book and then working to get it published. It was all so exciting then. At the same time, she could still recall how lonely she'd felt on the morning that her first book was officially published, and then later that day when she attended the publication party that was written up in *The New York Times*. She had been accompanied by her parents and close girlfriends, but there had been no special man in her life.

As she continued dressing for her return appearance, she recalled how blessed she had felt when, at thirty-six, she was introduced to Greg by a mutual friend. She remembered the first time they met and the breathlessness she'd felt when she saw him, so impressive-looking, handsome and tall, wearing a distinctive black wool, floor-length coat. But best of all, he was searching for the same things she was—someone to marry and with whom to start a family.

They talked until the wee hours of the morning that first date and then she took a cab home. They went out again the next day, and the day after that.

That same week, her cousin Monica was getting married. Emily took a taxi to the wedding in Glen Rock, New Jersey and met her parents at the chapel.

"I just met someone I really like," she whispered to her father as they waited for the ceremony to begin.

She paused a moment for her father to turn to her mother and share the news with her.

"There's only one thing," she added. "He's not Jewish."

"Oh, is that all," her father answered.

By that point in Emily's life, her father no longer cared if her boyfriend was of the same religion. It was a far cry from when he had forbidden her to see the high school boy she lost her virginity to because (among other things) he wasn't Jewish. But then, a lot had happened in the ensuing years. Emily's first brief marriage, at the age of twenty, didn't work out, and her first husband was Jewish. Around that same time, her older brother had been murdered, and a part of her father had died with his son. By the time Emily met Greg, her parents had basically given up on her ever settling down again. Her boyfriends' religious propensities just didn't seem as important anymore.

A WEEK AFTER HER COUSIN'S WEDDING, Emily was supposed to go out with her parents for her birthday. But at the last minute they called and canceled, explaining that they had just seen her the week before at her cousin's wedding.

Emily felt devastated by her parents' decision not to see her twice in one week and saddened by the thought of spending her birthday alone. But then Greg called and comforted her by saying, "Great! Now *I* can take you out for your birthday. What would you like to do?"

"I'd like to go to a Broadway show," Emily replied, secretly thinking that if Greg was really as enamored of her as he seemed, this would be a test of his true feelings.

Greg passed the test, getting orchestra seats to Bernadette Peters starring in *Sunday in the Park With George*, and then showing up at Emily's apartment door with a birthday present, a hardcover edition of *Evil Under the Sun* by one of his favorite writers, Agatha Christie, that he had tracked down at a secondhand bookstore on 13th Street in the West Village.

Emily didn't know it, but Greg had decided that if she quit smoking, he was going to ask her to marry him. That would be no small accomplishment for Emily, who had been a chain smoker since her divorce at the age of 23. She was up to more than three packs a day. The only time she wasn't smoking was when she was sleeping, and then she would dream that she was smoking.

Greg, who had stopped smoking himself years before, declared his love for her, but made it clear to Emily that he would never marry someone who smoked. One morning soon after, Emily woke up in Greg's apartment after they spent the night together. She went into the refrigerator and got a container of yogurt and began eating it for breakfast. She was already smoking her first cigarette of the day, often the most important one, the one to get the nicotine back into her lungs and blood stream so she wouldn't experience the mini-withdrawal that she went through every day between going to bed and that first cigarette upon awakening.

But that morning, instead of finishing the cigarette, she plunged the half-smoked filter cigarette into the container of blueberry yogurt, and flung the package into the kitchen garbage can.

There were many hugs and reassuring affirmations from Greg over the next few days, as they stayed together with Emily often delirious from withdrawal along with the rage and longing that quitting cold turkey had brought out.

But she didn't waver. Emily was 135 pounds when she quit smoking, a size 5/7. Cigarettes had helped her to control her appetite and deal with a lifelong battle with food. If Emily had a cigarette and a cup of coffee, she was satisfied. She kept almost no food in her refrigerator and only ate a normal dinner if she had a date. The rest of the time, she would just nibble. For years, she had kept her weight down by also fasting every Monday, to make up for the additional eating she did over the weekends when she socialized.

Chain smoking was a very big part of her weight control regime, as well as working out at the health club with her friend

Kathleen, who kept her weight down by eating just one fourth of every portion on her plate.

Emily had been smoking steadily since the age of sixteen, except for those three years of her first marriage, and it defined the way she dealt with anxiety. Although she had her first cigarette during her senior year of high school, it was during her freshman year of college, when she was sixteen, that smoking became a habit. When Emily finally quit, she had to readjust the way she negotiated the world. She needed to find other ways to deal with frustration and hunger, rage, anxiety, and nervousness.

Three days after her last cigarette, on December 25th, Greg met Emily's parents at the Hilton. Afterwards, Greg rented a car and they drove upstate to meet Greg's parents and celebrate Christmas with them. Emily was amazed that they arrived at noon and stayed till almost seven since she had rarely spent more than an hour or two at a time with her parents in all her adult years. There was Greg's sister Susan and her two teenage daughters; his Mom and Dad, in their late fifties; and his Mom's sister, a schoolteacher who never married and lived nearby and who always spent the holidays with her sister and her family. Greg's great-uncle and great-aunt lived next door, so Emily got to meet them as well. They did not spend any time in Greg's parents' home because Greg's father, mother, and sister were smokers, and the smoke bothered his aunt and uncle.

"Want a cigarette?" Greg's father asked Emily.

"Dad, Emily just quit smoking," Greg replied.

"Let her talk for herself," Greg's father persisted. "So, do you want a cigarette or not? One can't hurt you."

"No, thanks," Emily said, smiling, trying to hide the deep longing and craving she had for that cigarette. It was so hard for her to be in that living room filled with cigarette smoke, but she didn't want to make a fuss. This family reunion was too important to Greg and she didn't want to ruin it by demanding that they leave early because her withdrawal symptoms were returning in the presence of secondary smoke.

On the way back to Manhattan, just minutes after leaving his childhood home, Greg pulled off the narrow one-lane country road, near an old gas station, and asked Emily, "Will you marry me?"

"Yes," was Emily's simple reply, sealed with a long, deep, wet and passionate kiss.

Six days later, they got their blood tests and marriage license. They had planned on getting married at City Hall, but when they saw the couples waiting in line to get married, it looked like such a sad way to begin a new married life together. They wanted their beginning to be festive, filled with close family as well as the friends they cared about who had helped both of them through all those single years. So on a Friday they began calling their friends and nearest relatives, advising them that they were getting married that Sunday in the Manhattan loft of Greg's friend Dave.

Together Greg and Emily shopped for the champagne, cheese, chocolates, strawberries, and paper goods that they would need for the wedding. Emily's close friend Barbara accompanied her to a plush Fifth Avenue department store where Emily found a gorgeous sample wedding dress that fit her perfectly. It was the first time Emily paid $825 for a dress but it had been reduced from $3,000 and it was just the right look, color, and style. There was the added benefit of Emily being a perfect size 7 so no alterations were needed.

Barbara found a rabbi to perform the ceremony as well as two musicians to play chamber music until it began. Emily's cousin Tom asked a friend who owed him a favor to be the wedding photographer. Her sister and brother-in-law came up from Chevy Chase, Maryland, as did Greg's mother (she said his father was sick), aunt, sister, and most of their closest friends assembled in that loft. Seventy-five people, including several babies and toddlers, gathered with just 36 hours' notice to watch Greg and Emily join their lives together.

EMILY THOUGHT THAT GREG was the most caring, emotionally honest man she had ever met. She was so impressed with how insightful he was that, early in their marriage, she wanted to begin seeing his therapist, Dr. Herbert Peters. Greg had explained he needed someone "objective" to talk to, as he put it, someone "safe" to confide in and work through the aftermath of a distant relationship with his parents during his formative years.

Greg knew that his earliest experiences made it harder for him to trust people but he had emotionally opened up considerably from his years in therapy. So, within a week of getting married, Emily began a therapeutic relationship with Dr. Peters that endured, and strengthened, from that first moment until Dr. Peters' death, fourteen years later.

It was through the work Emily did with Dr. Peters that so much of her healing had occurred. He was the first therapist, out of four, who helped her to talk about the roots of her anxiety and addiction to nicotine and then, after the chain-smoking ended, to the compulsive overeating that replaced the cigarettes, or the "deadly nipple," as Greg called them.

She was seeking alternatives to a steady diet of sucking candies (a much sweeter nipple) and lollipops, or to munching on pretzels and peanuts, which she used to replace her three-pack a day habit—when she learned she was pregnant.

SUDDENLY, PUTTING AN END to her compulsive overeating was no longer Emily's focus. Consuming a balanced diet, taking her vitamins, and doing whatever she could to have a healthy baby became pivotal. Only somehow she convinced herself that thick ice cream milk shakes would ensure that she was getting enough calcium and her baby would be born healthy. The quadruple-digit calorie count of each milk shake was not her concern; it was all for the baby growing inside her.

Being a compulsive worrier, Emily was far more frantic about the pregnancy than Greg who, exuding his usual calm and hopefulness, felt confident that everything would go well. The sonogram and then the amniocentesis all indicated that they were having a healthy boy.

Still, Emily worried every minute of her pregnancy, playing negative "what if" scenarios in her mind. She made pacts with God that if she could just have a healthy baby, "I'll never use another foul word again." "I'll stop complaining about the little insignificant things in life." "I'll do a good deed a day for the rest of my life."

And with every month of her pregnancy, Emily gained 10 pounds rather than the total of 25 for the entire pregnancy that her OB/GYN recommended.

"Every pound you gain over twenty-five is yours to keep," her obstetrician warned.

Yes, she was piling on the weight, reinforcing the compulsive overeating habits that she had developed since quitting smoking, week after week after week. But Emily deluded herself that she wasn't really "that fat" and that it was all tied to her pregnancy.

By the time Emily was seven months pregnant, when her belly was big enough for Greg and her to finally believe that their baby was going to soon become a reality, they discussed possible childcare arrangements.

"Whatever you want to do is fine with me," Greg said matter-of-factly.

"But don't you want me to stay home, full-time?" Emily asked.

"Of course."

"I mean since you were raised by emotionally distant and preoccupied parents, and sent to stay with your relatives for weeks at a time, and I was basically raised by a cleaning lady, don't we want something different for our son?"

"Yes."

"So why did you say it's up to me?"

"Because you're the one who'll be staying home," Greg replied. "So you've got to be fine with it. I'll go along with whatever you decide."

Boy, this was a different way of handling decisions than the way it was when Emily was a child or during her brief first marriage. "There's a right way and a wrong way and the right way is my way," was the message she received while growing up and then into her first marriage.

At her next therapy session, Emily told Dr. Peters what Greg had said. Dr. Peters listened, silently.

Then Emily started to talk about how it felt to be convinced that she was raised more by Dolores, their cleaning lady, than by her own mother.

DOLORES CAME TO WORK FOR her parents when Emily was two—and she would stay for twenty-five years. Dolores, who was black and a widow, lived with her son and daughter. Another daughter had been raped and murdered before Dolores came to work for Emily's parents, Dr. and Mrs. Keane, but they never knew any of the details about how it happened. Dolores took care of the house and did all the cooking. She never took the children anywhere or played games with them, but she was usually alone in the house with them. She was not really a nanny; she was what was then called "full-time help" or a "maid."

Emily told her therapist how almost all the warm memories she had of Dolores, of making ice box cakes with dozens of chocolate wafers and thick cream that Dolores would whip with a beater, full breakfasts with two eggs, bacon, buttered toast, and tea with lots of milk, were food-related.

Almost all of Emily's childhood memories of being nurtured—having her long brown hair braided before school, being taken care of when she was sick, or having roses cut from her backyard bushes to bring to her teachers—were of Dolores, not her mother. Dolores didn't talk very much, but she gave Emily the best "bear hugs."

She remembered how ineffective Dolores had been at protecting her or her sister Dora when their brother tried to beat them up whenever their mother would help out at their father's medical office. Martin would jump on top of Dora and Emily, pinning them down, one at a time, on the carpeted living room floor. Dora and Emily would ultimately win those fights if they worked together to gang up on their older brother. Until they were winning the fight, however, Emily would hide behind Dolores, as she stood at the kitchen sink in her formal maid's black uniform and white apron.

But Emily recalled that having Dolores there was like having no one. The three of them would fight and run around. The leadership in the house wasn't really there.

The memories came rushing back as pregnant Emily, already 180 pounds, a far cry from her wedding weight of 135, sat in the big leather chair in her therapist's upper West Side office, her swollen feet elevated on a tiny wooden foot stool.

"If Dolores hadn't been there, my mother would have," Emily said, with amazement. The lower lids of her eyes felt wet with tears, and her knees flinched as her entire body responded to the magnitude of her realization.

She was determined to make different choices for her unborn child. Although having a nanny might work fine for others, it was not an option Emily wanted to pursue.

In reality, if Dolores hadn't been there, thought Emily, social services would have intervened. She felt saddened by the thought that even the threat of having her children taken away might not have given her mother the motivation she needed to physically and emotionally make herself available during the day for her children.

EMILY RESIGNED HERSELF TO either giving up or at least winding down her private practice and definitely leaving her full-time teaching job to raise their baby. It was not an easy choice. She had worked long and hard to get her doctorate and then, despite a very tight market, to find herself a full-time assistant professorship. She was already 37, far older than most entry-level academicians, so she actually needed to play "catch up" if she were to get her academic career to the place it should be. She had also toiled long hours to build up her therapy practice. She had at least a half-dozen regular clients that she saw once or twice a week, plus several participants in her two weekly group therapy sessions.

But she was about to be a first-time mother and she had to consider the needs of her unborn child first.

Little did Emily know how difficult the decision to be there full-time as a mother was going to be, emotionally and professionally. She also wasn't prepared for how little support she received from her parents and the new mothers she befriended who seemed to accept that they would return to work full time. The main supporters of her decision were Greg, her therapist, Dr. Peters, and her oldest childhood friend, Sally.

Sally was her former next-door neighbor, who had resisted any pressure to return too soon to teaching, because the family needed the money, until her son and daughter were at an age that Sally felt her presence at home was less necessary.

Emily's sister Dora was promoted while she was out on maternity leave, and returned to work when her daughter was five months old, hiring a full-time nanny who stayed for the next seven years.

"Then again, my sister and I disagree about how lonely and empty our childhood was," Emily explained to Dr. Peters.

"She never minded our mother's emotional distance those first ten years, or her physical distance once she had her full-time job. But my sister was almost two years older than me."

WHEN EMILY GAVE BIRTH TO her son Doug she weighed 217 pounds. Although she dropped to 200 soon afterwards, she stayed at that weight for more than a year.

It had been a battle over the next fifteen years to lose, and keep off, those extra pounds. But finally she did it. She had traded all the prestige, stimulation, and paycheck of a career in clinical psychology for the love of an infant who initially couldn't do anything but cry, breastfeed, sleep, and ask for constant attention. Only to be followed, three years later, by a second son, Stan.

Now she was finally heading into Manhattan in a town car to a network TV show. She was back to her wedding weight of 135 and had a best-selling new book to promote called *Forgotten Intimacy*. It had been a long struggle but she felt as if she were being rewarded for her choices, decisions, and sacrifices over those fifteen years, especially the first ten when she had turned down every offer for paid travel for business, no matter how alluring or how high the fee, if it meant staying away even one night from her children. She also did not pursue professional opportunities if it meant taking too much attention away from her children, such as major TV appearances. Unlike some mothers who could juggle careers and still care for very young children, Emily knew her limitations.

When both her children were in full-time elementary school, Emily found herself with the entire school day to pursue her own career goals. She was surprised at how hard it was for her to recall how grueling it had been for all those months, then years, after giving up her practice to "stay home." Initially, her productivity dipped to almost nothing. Being a full-time mother consumed her and she had not yet learned how to provide therapy to her clients or to write within short blocks of time, as she would train herself to do.

Emily kept busy and eventually brought in some income by seeing clients on an occasional basis. She also created writing projects related to motherhood including a book on *What to Do with Your Baby*, and a proposal for a book entitled *How to Stay Home (Temporarily) and Love It* (which she couldn't sell back then since it was an unpopular but traditional concept that was becoming new again but Emily was about ten years ahead of its rebirth), as well as a word book documenting in original drawings or photographs each word that her son Doug said, and the date upon which he first uttered it. She also wrote several poems and got magazine and book assignments from time to time.

Emily could not have guessed that it would be almost a decade later when, with their second son in elementary school and Emily's fertility coming to a halt, that she could return to writing in such a concerted way that a major morning talk show would, once again, seek her out for her expertise and book authorship.

ALL THOSE THOUGHTS FLASHED through Emily's mind as she and Greg hugged and kissed beside the town car waiting to take her into Manhattan and to *The Morning Show.*

It was five a.m., but Emily was wide-awake. She had had trouble sleeping the night before, worrying, of course, about whether or not the car would even show up.

It was better to be early than late, she reminded herself. As the car pulled away from the driveway, she wondered, looking at Greg retreating back inside the house, why she hadn't begged her mother to come watch the boys so Greg could accompany her to the show. Every celebrity she had ever met at a talk show in the past always had someone, at least one person, along to provide support or conversation: a publicist, a friend, a family member.

During the 45-minute ride into Manhattan, she thought back to the first time she did *The Morning Show* and how the publishing company's publicist had accompanied her. She used to think it was out of respect for her and her work, but then she realized it was such a major coup to get an author on one of the three major network morning talk shows that it was good for the publicist to accompany the author. In that way, the publicist could keep that connection going, to say hello to the producers and the hosts, to be a face that succeeds in placing authors—not just another face-less publishing company lackey, hoping that her phone calls would get returned, her press releases read, and her authors booked.

This time, Emily was on her own. The booking came directly to her because the producer had read an interview Emily gave about her book to *USA Today.* Emily had actually enjoyed having direct communication with the producer and her staff, until today. Now she wished she had the support staff of her publisher or of her family to go with her and get her through this experience, even if it was just Greg.

Just Greg. Who was she kidding? Greg would have been more than enough. Greg was her life, besides their sons. Greg validated Emily in a way that nothing and no one had ever done before, not her writing, not her parents, not her siblings, not her friends. Oh, yes, everyone that mattered to Emily gave her something, some big or little thing, that enhanced her self-esteem, made her feel as if she counted, but it was always a little bit of that, and a little bit of this.

Greg seemed to appreciate every aspect of Emily: her mind, her talents, her beauty, and her sensuality. She could share each and every secret with him and there were no negative consequences. Putting it simply: he didn't judge her. He did not make her feel fearful, as her parents had done. He did not betray her, as her sister had unwittingly done when she told her parents that her sister had lost her virginity causing a whole series of negative consequences including Emily's mandatory separation from her boyfriend and beginning treatment with a questionable psychiatrist her father found in the telephone directory.

If only she had met Greg in those earlier, formative years, so much might have been different. Or maybe she was not ready until thirty-six? Maybe Emily had to punish herself or experience so many negative relationships that she would recognize the real thing when she finally found it, and do whatever it would take to hold on to that relationship, and to that family life, and make it work—not throw it away because of laziness, stupidity, or just plain ignorance about how rare it is to be loved and love, as so many do, and even Emily had done once in her early twenties. She had certainly thrown away potentially worthwhile relationships more than once.

As she looked at herself in her size 7 suit, Emily thought how no one would have suspected that she ever had a weight problem. She not only looked trim and fit but comfortable in that skin, as if she always looked that way.

Emily gave the appearance of confidence that morning on the way to an interview that would last for all of seven minutes and be seen by more than five million men and women. She looked successful. She exuded self-assurance. She was happily married, accomplished in her field, a Ph.D. from a well-regarded university that had graduated nuclear scientists, statesmen, and Pulitzer Prize winning authors. She looked far younger than her fifty years.

This was the moment she had been working toward for twenty-five years: a return performance to a major morning network talk show, the biggest of the original "Big Three" network giants. Yes, it had been an incredible accomplishment to be interviewed on *The Oprah Winfrey Show* six months earlier, and definitely one of the highlights of her career. Emily had been interviewed on Oprah because of her expertise as well as her authorship of a book on the topic that she was also discussing today: intimacy. But on *Oprah* she was situated in the studio audience, brought in for a few minutes as an expert halfway through the show, conversing with Oprah, but not sharing the stage with her. Although Emily did get to meet Oprah at the end of the show, and held her hand for several minutes, feeling the energy and strength of the media mogul, the focus of the show was on Oprah, the topic, and the guests. Emily was just one segment in an entire hour devoted to intimacy.

But this morning, Dr. Emily Taylor was going one-on-one with one of the most powerful women in morning network news. It was going to be Emily and Rosalie Brewster, and she was excited to be right there with millions watching as they engaged in an exclusive interview on intimacy that allowed Emily to share her thoughts and knowledge with all those viewers. Immediately, she began to worry about whether she going to inspire and educate those viewers, or bore them to tears?

EMILY WAS NOW IN WHAT was called "the green room," the room where they placed the guests before they go on the show. She recalled from her earlier days that she had to avoid sharing her key points with other guests in the green room. She had seen too many novices chit-chat about what they were *planning* to say later on, once they were on air, only to leave out the best examples or ideas when they actually did the interview. Was it a fear of repeating themselves, or simply an example of "been there, done that?" Whatever the reason, Emily had learned to save everything related to the focus of the interview for when actually doing the interview, whether taped or live.

As she waited to go on, she remembered another reason she liked doing the major morning shows. They always had excellent make-up artists and hairdressers; and, the green rooms were well-stocked with coffee, tea, juice, bagels and cream cheese, pastries, fresh fruit, and bottles of water. This morning's green room was already set up when Emily arrived, a full hour early, the first guest in the room. To keep her mind off the food, she made small talk with the usher.

"How'd you get this job?" Emily asked.

"I worked here as an intern last summer and they said I could come back when I graduated, so I did," he explained.

"It must be exciting," Emily replied.

Emily finally walked over to the lavish spread of food. For a moment, her hand touched a bagel, but she quickly pulled it away and grabbed a piece of sliced cantaloupe instead. She took another cup of coffee, counting to herself how many cups she had had so far. She didn't want to overdo it. She didn't want to be too jittery by the time she was interviewed.

A couple entered the room surrounded by three other people including the talent booker and a publicist attached to the show. The couple and the man accompanying them looked vaguely familiar to Emily. They appeared to be a husband and wife but the husband was shorter than he had seemed on television. The woman looked a bit heavier, maybe by about ten pounds, but she was still quite lovely. Emily seemed to recall that the man accompanying them was their lawyer; then she realized where she had seen that couple before. They had become famous because their beautiful young daughter had been kidnapped and murdered and for a while they had been considered prime suspects. Emily figured they were in their mid-fifties or early sixties. It was hard to tell. Stress and public scrutiny had taken their toll.

"Hi, I'm Sarah Towers," the stunning woman said to Emily as she extended her hand.

"Emily Taylor," she replied, shaking Mrs. Towers' hand.

"I'm sure you know why we're here," said Mrs. Towers. "How about you?"

"I'm here to talk about my book, *Forgotten Intimacy*," said Emily. "I've spent the last decade researching intimacy and whether Americans are more connected or disconnected today."

"I'm Charles Towers," the man said, extending his hand to Emily.

"I'm so sorry for your loss," Emily blurted out.

As often as Emily had met celebrities in the past, there was still that little-girl fascination with those who were made by the media to seem larger than life. They looked like such a kind and caring couple. Emily found it hard to believe any of the allegations that either of them had anything to do with the horrific murder five years before of their talented and adorable daughter, four-year-old Clarissa.

"I also wrote a book about crime victims," Emily shared. "My brother was the victim of a street mugging, a homicide," she added.

Sarah Towers expressed her condolences at Emily's loss.

"We're not allowed to be victims," Sarah Towers then said to Emily.

Emily offered to send the Towers a book that she had co-authored about dealing with grief. Mrs. Towers eagerly accepted the offer and wrote her mailing address, a post office box in Minnesota, in Emily's notebook so Emily could follow up.

MEETING THE TOWERS DISTRACTED Emily from preparing her thoughts about intimacy, and ushered her back thirty years to what had happened to her older brother Martin. It was March fifth, a Tuesday, a day burned into her memory forever, details clinging to her mind like dust on a shelf of books high up and never cleaned. Emily could still see how she looked that day with her long, thick, waist-length dark hair, beautiful, a pretty twenty-year-old with a nice figure, excited and nervous about her upcoming wedding a week later. It was early evening when her mother called. Emily had just returned from a full day of classes at Tyler University out on Long Island where she was a senior.

"Martin's been stabbed," her mother said.

"What?"

"Martin's been stabbed," her mother repeated.

There was a long pause.

"It looks bad," she added.

Emily's mother filled her in on what had happened. Apparently, Martin had been approached by three teenagers somewhere between 42nd and 43rd Street and Ninth Avenue in Manhattan, around 11 o'clock the night before. (In all these years, Emily thought, she'd never asked her parents *why* they didn't call her, or her sister, as soon as it happened.)

The police had taken Martin to the nearest hospital after finding him slumped over his steering wheel about twenty blocks away from where the stabbing occurred. It seemed Martin had been trying to drive himself to the hospital when, because of his wounds, he could not go any further.

Her parents got a call at around 11:30 with the news. They picked up Martin's wife Melanie and went to the hospital. Their family physician and friend, Dr. Katz, met them there.

"While the doctors were attending to Martin's wounds, they spoke to us. They said Martin was going to be okay. Dr. Katz even confirmed their diagnosis. They said the wounds were superficial. We all thought Martin was going to be fine. Dr. Katz even said to us, 'Well, it's a stab wound. At least it's not a bullet with peritonitis.'"

Emily's mother said she'd asked Martin what happened.

"I can't understand it," Martin had told her. "What fools," he said. "I offered them my wallet. They didn't want it. I can't understand it. I can't understand it. There were three of them. They asked me for two dimes and before I had a chance to give it to them I got stabbed."

"Mom, what's happened since last night?"

"We left Martin at the hospital because they said he'd be fine, that the wounds were superficial. So we drove Melanie back to her apartment. Then we came home to go to sleep. We were exhausted. It must have been two, three o'clock in the morning by then."

"Then what?"

"So we went back around noon today. We sat all day and no one had the courtesy to tell us that my son was in surgery."

It was not until 4 or 5 o'clock that next day, frantic, after her father again complained, "I can't find out a thing about our son," that the surgeon said, "His liver is half or three-quarters gone. We might get a liver machine, but that often doesn't work."

It was only when they realized how grave the situation was that Emily's parents decided to call her. Emily was in a frenzied state as she listened to her mother. She felt overwrought with a combination of emotions□ worry about her brother along with fear, shock, and disbelief, as well as anger that they hadn't called right away.

She promised her mother she would ask Tom, her fiancé, to take her to the hospital so she would not have to go out alone at night. Emily felt ashamed that she continued to lie to her parents about her living arrangements. Even though she and Tom had been engaged for several months, Emily was still afraid of her parents' disapproval. In the midst of this crisis, she kept up the masquerade that Tom was living further uptown in his own apartment.

As Emily got off the phone, Tom, who had been patiently sitting next to her throughout the conversation, asked anxiously, "Is it your father? Has he had a heart attack?"

"No."

"Your grandmother?"

"No."

She hugged Tom and began crying in his arms.

"It's my brother Martin. He's been stabbed."

Before Emily left to go to the hospital, she suddenly wondered if her hair looked good. It bothered her that she could be concerned with her appearance at such a time.

The first people Emily and Tom met when they arrived at the hospital were her cousin Rachel and her aunt, her mother's younger sister. How could they get here so quickly, Emily wondered, since they had to travel from Long Island—unless her mother had called them before she even told Emily?

Her thoughts quickly faded as she took in the image of her father holding his dark brown hat in his hands. When he saw Emily, he began to cry. That was the first time in her entire life Emily had seen her father cry. His outpouring of feeling and emotion stunned Emily. Then she reeled in her frustration that she did not know what to do or say to comfort him.

At that moment, she knew that her older brother must be dying.

But she put that thought out of her head and instead worked furiously to try to gain control of the situation. She remembered getting on the phone and trying to find out how to get Martin moved to a private hospital. It seemed they were caught in a bureaucratic situation since the police had initially taken him to City Hospital. But Emily was also assured that the surgeons, residents and interns who operated on her brother at the city hospital were the same ones who would have treated him at the affiliated private one. She also learned there was only one surgeon at that time who had successfully repaired livers damaged to the extent her brother's was and he lived in California. She didn't know why she didn't pursue that possibility any further, perhaps because it was already too late. But the trusting and, in hindsight, ineffective way everyone reacted to Martin's medical crisis always haunted Emily with the "what ifs."

They told Emily that Martin had lost a lot of blood and that he needed more blood for the additional operations. He was type O+, not rare but a less common type of blood, so that was what she focused on, not the possibility that her brother would probably die. She went out to Tyler University in Garden City, Long Island and visited each and every one of her classes, getting permission from her professors to make an announcement to her fellow classmates, asking anyone with O+ blood to donate it. She provided instructions on how to donate it and make sure it actually got to her brother at City Hospital. She called up any of Martin's high school or college friends she could remember and asked them to donate blood.

"Is Paul there?"

"Who's calling?"

"This is Martin Keane's sister. Paul went to high school with my brother. They were friends."

"Yes, I remember. What do you want?"

"My brother has been stabbed. He's in the hospital and

needs blood donations."

"I'm sorry but Paul has a job interview tomorrow. I'm not going to tell him anything that might upset him tonight," and Paul's father hung up the phone. Shocked at the response, Emily began dialing the next name on her list. Most gave her excuses why they couldn't help, but a few came through.

The night Martin was stabbed he had gone to a show at a comedy club with a friend. They went back to his friend's apartment in the Murray Hill section of Manhattan and ate some sandwiches. His friend said he watched Martin go out the front door to his car, a small blue foreign model parked nearby, as snow blanketed the streets. But he said he didn't actually see Martin get into his car. Nor did he see him get stabbed.

Emily wanted to ask Martin what exactly had happened but he was already unconscious by the time her parents called her to the hospital. He never regained consciousness. It turned out a gang of teenagers had a clubhouse nearby where they used to practice inserting their knives into dummies, the kind that fighters use to work out on, twisting the knife so it would lacerate the liver or other organs, increasing the likelihood that the victim would die, thus decreasing the chance of an eye witness who could identify the muggers.

At that point, her family had very little information about what happened to Martin, or why. As the doctors fought to save his life, another young man, also twenty-three and from Queens, an artist who was living near 10th Avenue and 42nd Street, was similarly mugged and stabbed to death when he went out around eleven o'clock to buy a pack of cigarettes. It looked like the work of the same gang.

Years later, Emily interviewed one of the police officers who got the call over the radio car and brought Martin to the hospital. By then he had left police work and was doing construction.

"I'm speaking from the viewpoint of a human being," he told Emily over the phone. "I'm completely free of it all now. I don't owe anything to the city or the state of New York. Your brother had this incident sometime before midnight. Change of tour at midnight. At that time, you couldn't get a cop between ten-to-twelve until ten-after-twelve. Everyone knew it. Also, Times Square especially over by Tenth Avenue was a bad scene during those years. The young kids who moved into that area attracted a lot of shit along with them."

Emily remembered spending the next night at her parents' house in Queens. At that point, her older sister Dora still had not been told what had happened to their brother. Every time Emily brought up calling her sister at the exclusive college she was attending, her parents begged her not to. "Don't worry her," they would say, as if by not telling Dora, this would all go away. It was as if they were waiting to be able to tell her only good news.

When Emily realized good news would not be forthcoming, she sneaked into her father's den, the room that used to be her brother's when they were growing up, and she called her sister.

"If you want to see Martin before he dies, you'd better come right away," Emily said, choking on each word as she forced herself to state the obvious.

Dora was completely startled by the news, learning about what happened to Martin even later than Emily did.

"I'll find out how I can get there and when and let you know."

There was already six inches of snow cutting Dora's campus off from the car rides that would usually be offered on a Thursday for those who wanted to drive to Manhattan for a long weekend.

It was an 8-hour drive from the college campus to Manhattan; it was not accessible by plane or bus and Dora didn't have her own car or do much long-distance driving.

THE NEXT DAY, EMILY DONATED BLOOD. She hoped that since she was trying so hard to save Martin he would pull through. Then she got another thought that she was ashamed of, but it was there, nevertheless. She grew up feeling that Martin was the favored one, the one who got the most attention, and here he was, once again getting all the attention by getting stabbed and upstaging Emily's wedding that was to take place in just a week!

Now she had a new scenario that actually gave her some comfort because she might be able to control the outcome: Maybe it was her blood that would help him pull through. But when was that going to happen?

Emily spent many hours holding vigil in the cafeteria of the hospital with her cousins, aunt, and uncle. Why hadn't she demanded to at least go in and see her brother? Sure, he was still unconscious, but at least he was alive. She could have talked to him, even if he couldn't hear her. What a waste of time to be in that cafeteria socializing when her brother was dying all alone in some room in an old, run-down city hospital.

Emily's sister Dora finally arrived early the next evening. She went right to their parents' house. The hospital no longer needed more O+ blood for Martin.

The next morning, five days after the attack, they went back to the hospital.

"He's brain dead," the resident explained.

Emily's parents, accompanied by Martin's wife, Melanie, and her parents, explained to Emily and Dora that Martin was a vegetable, kept alive only on life support.

"So, why not keep him alive until he can be healed?" asked Emily.

"His liver can't be repaired," said the Doctor. "Basically, he's a vegetable."

"But he's still alive," said Emily.

"With no hope of recovery," said the Doctor. "I'm very sorry."

Emily took Dora's hand and together, their hands and legs trembling, they walked into Martin's hospital room to say good-bye.

Emily saw her brother, his skin more white than real, hooked up to machines and surrounded by white sheets. She wished she could think of something profound to say; some thought to help her sister or herself through this. Instead, she said, simply, "Good-bye, Martin."

She cried quietly and began to shake. Her knees and legs were weak but she still managed to maintain control.

✦

LOOKING BACK, EMILY REALIZED as she sat in the green room, she had reacted far more maturely than her twenty years should have allowed in the face of such a horrific crime and tragedy and personal loss.

What she wasn't prepared for were the overwhelming feelings of rage and guilt she would later feel, feelings that fed into the hunger that drove her toward the food she used to calm those feelings and satisfy an insatiable need.

AFTER SAYING THEIR GOODBYES, Emily, her sister, and her fiancé went back to her parents' home and she remembered that night it was very hard to get to sleep. Her fiancé stayed in the basement and Emily slept on the sofa bed in the family room with her sister Dora and her cousin beside her. They were afraid. None of them had ever lost a family member this close before. A grandfather and a step-grandmother had died, but they were either too young to really remember, or they had not formed a close bond. This was different. Not only were they close to their brother, but he was a peer, a contemporary. Until then death was something very far away, something that only happened to very old and sick people or to political martyrs, like JFK or Martin Luther King.

Emily's brother's death was so final and so unlike the happy ending she had worked out in her mind to comfort herself.

"Martin, it wasn't supposed to end like this," she remembered saying to herself. "You were supposed to pull through. That was the way it was should have turned out."

She later learned that they caught the gang responsible for killing her brother and the second young man. The gang had tried to commit a third mugging when one of the victims fought back and was able to identify his attackers to the police.

Eventually the gang was tried and two were convicted for the homicide of the artist, the second homicide victim. The assistant district attorney and the police were confident they were the assailants in Emily's brother's case, although it never came to trial since they had been tried, and convicted, for the other murder.

The day after her brother died, Martin had to be autopsied because he had been the victim of a homicide. So at two o'clock in the afternoon, her fiancé accompanied her father to identify Martin's body.

Emily's fiancé Tom told her that when he and her father returned to her parents' house, he saw the leather jacket and pants that Martin had been wearing when he was stabbed.

"There were bloodstains everywhere," said Tom. "I could see the places where the stiletto had gone through the jacket. Your father put the jacket in the garage because he didn't want you or your mother to see it."

Whatever information Emily learned about what might have happened to her brother was through talking to a reporter at the *LaGuardia Times*. The Sunday after Martin died, one-column articles also appeared in the two major New York newspapers. These reiterated the same information as the *LaGuardia Times* but added a few mistakes which seemed so important at the time, like writing that her brother had a daughter, when he really had a son and one on the way; but now, looking back, seemed so meaningless.

Emily remembered how they spent the time from Friday, when Martin was declared dead, until his viewing on Saturday night making phone calls to friends and relatives, telling them that Martin had died, a mugging victim, and that the viewing was Saturday night and the funeral on Sunday. Martin and his wife's next-door neighbors were helping out by going through Martin's phone book and calling everyone who was not a close relative. But they missed the mark next to Martin's grandmother's name that indicated "do not call" and telephoned the old woman anyway.

"Martin Keane has been killed. The funeral is Sunday," they told Martin's grandmother in Florida.

The woman became hysterical and called Emily's mother.

"No, Mom," her mother explained. "It must have been some

kind of a crank caller. Everything is fine. We just want you to come up a week early to get ready for Emily's wedding. That's all."

Emily's parents had decided it was better to tell her grandmother in person about what had happened to her grandson.

Martin's viewing was packed with hundreds of friends and relatives. They were all frozen in shock and horror over how he had died. Thirty years ago, the murder of a twenty-three-year-old middle-class boy was far less common than, sadly, it would be considered today. The casket was open and Emily remembered thinking how unfair it was that those who had not seen Martin in a long time would remember him always in the bloated, overweight, and inhuman way he now appeared. She wished she had brought along a photograph of her brother when he was thinner, reminding them of how handsome he really was when he was alive and vital, and not filled with whatever fluids the embalmer put in, or the horrific assault on his physical appearance after enduring an autopsy.

Emily remembered how strong her sister-in-law Melanie was, just like Jacqueline Kennedy had been when President Kennedy was slain in Texas. Emily tried to be strong, like Melanie, and only cried when she saw someone from her brother's past, someone she knew deeply cared about him.

The next morning, Sunday, the day of the funeral, the snow started falling, lightly at first, three inches by nine. By eleven, when the funeral took place, there was already four inches. Emily's friend Clara called from Providence to let her know that she couldn't get a flight out because of the snow. There was a smaller crowd at the funeral because of the snow but it was still overflowing with local mourners.

The rabbi who delivered the eulogy was the one who had presided over Martin's Bar Mitzvah. The casket was displayed in front of the enormous chapel with a huge floor-to-ceiling window behind it. You could see the snow falling as a backdrop to the rabbi's words:

"My dear family members and friends. It is clear from the standing room-only crowd in this room today that Martin was beloved by many. Death is difficult to cope with whatever the age of the dearly departed for there is no age that is old enough to lose our loved ones to the great unknown. But when the deceased is so young, like Martin, it is that much more challenging not to feel despair. And when the death is caused by such a violent, senseless, and hateful act, it seems almost beyond our comprehension that this should happen or that we shall ever recover from the pain and loss that we are feeling today.

Martin's family members and his beloved friends, it may sound cruel for me to talk about the days ahead that may someday be bright again. Or that you will all be rewarded for continuing to believe despite the great test that Martin's death is asking of you. But I know that if you can just accept what has happened without trying to find a reason for it, that you will someday smile again. That you and your loved ones will someday feel joy and laughter even though you may now wonder if you will ever laugh at a joke or even want to dance or sing. The pain you are enduring may even seem unbearable but you can bear it.

And remember that Martin is not gone forever. He lives within the hearts of each one of you. He lives in the life of his seven-year-old child that he had been raising with his wife Melanie as well as their unborn son who will always be part of him and who will be born in just a few more months.

For their sake, for your sake, celebrate Martin's life, not his tragic death. Share your fond memories of Martin with each other and most of all with his family. Let his child and children and his widow know that Martin will never be forgotten. Send his children and his wife, and his mother, father, and sisters, a card in the years ahead, or call and say hello. Do not let this day be the end of your connection to Martin and his family and other friends.

May Martin's soul be bound up in the bond of eternal life. Amen."

The beauty of the snow falling outside contrasted with the

horrific circumstances of her brother's death. The tragedy was multiplied by his young age, by his wife being six months' pregnant, and by the fact that Martin had been a father to his wife's seven-year-old son for the last four years. It all left an indelible impression on the hundreds of mourners.

The snow had progressively worsened by the end of the service. The coating outside was deeper now and visibility was severely diminished. Only the hearse with the coffin and the car filled with Emily's parents, her sister, and the rabbi planned to drive out to the cemetery for the burial. Because of her condition, it was decided it was best if Martin's wife Melanie return to her apartment. Because of the blinding snow, it took almost two hours to drive to the cemetery, a trip that should have taken no more than an hour.

Once there, cemetery officials greeted the hearse with an announcement, "Sorry, but there are no burials today. The ground's frozen."

"What now?" Emily asked.

"We'll put the coffin in a secure place and bury your loved one as soon as we can after this snowstorm."

The long drive back took even longer as the snow piled as high as a foot on the side streets.

The Garden State Parkway was still moving, even though it was slow going.

Then, about ten miles from the cemetery, the road disappeared under a blanket of white. Cars were stranded and abandoned. Within minutes the parkway became a parking lot with cars unable to move in any direction.

It was bitter cold and because everyone in the hearse had been too consumed with grief to think about proper winter clothing, no one was really dressed for the frigid weather. The driver of the hearse, a tall man, was wearing boots. He got out of the car.

"Wait here," he said to Emily and her family and the rabbi.

"I'll look for a place for us to stay till the roads open up."

He was gone about five minutes.

"There's a new development not too far from here," he

explained. "The people who live in this one house said they would put us up for the night."

"But I don't have any boots," Dora said.

"Neither do I," Emily added.

"It's not too far," the driver assured them. "We can't stay here. We'll freeze to death."

One by one, they walked through the knee-deep snow, trying to put their feet in the indentations the driver had made since no one else had boots, stuffing their hands in their pockets since no one had any gloves.

By the time they got to the new house, their fingers felt frostbitten.

"My fingers, my fingers," Emily's mother cried, tears streaming down her face from the pain.

"Here," a woman in her mid-forties said to Mrs. Keane as she took her hands and started rubbing them. The woman was the owner of the house.

"Have some coffee," a young woman in her early twenties said, offering cups of coffee to the Keanes and their rabbi and the driver. She resembled the older woman and was probably her daughter.

Emily looked around as she got warmer. She noticed that in the basement of this almost finished home were at least twenty-five more people, all dressed in black or dark clothes. Their shared grief and their inability to bury their dead had united them. Stranded in a snowstorm they all huddled in this basement, sleeping in upright positions, but grateful to be inside and warm. During the night, Emily looked over at the rabbi as he began to lean over as if he was going to fall, but just before he did, he instinctively pulled himself up, and leaned to the other side.

The next day, the roads had still not been cleared. Emily, her parents, her sister, the rabbi, and the driver began walking toward home, which they now realized was about two miles up the road. After walking past a few more houses, they decided to stop at another house and see if they might borrow some dry clothes and add warmer clothes for the walk home.

"Cynthia," Emily screeched after the door of the house opened and the daughter of the homeowner appeared.

"Emily? Emily Keane!" Cynthia replied. "Come on in out of the cold!"

Emily explained to her parents that Cynthia was a classmate and friend from high school.

Twenty-five people died throughout New Jersey because of that snowstorm. Cars were stranded and ambulances couldn't get through. It was declared the worst storm in seventy-five years.

WITH THE FUNERAL AND THE SNOWSTORM behind them, the next question was, "What about Emily's wedding the following Sunday? What should we do now?"

Because of what had happened to Martin, Emily and her fiancé wanted to call off the wedding. But even more than that tragedy, they had been starting to feel that their impending union was a mistake, based on the wrong reasons. Tom was only getting married to please his parents. Emily was getting married because she didn't want to be alone. They were about to tell their families of their decision, when Emily's mother intervened.

"In the Jewish religion, you don't cancel something good because something bad happens," her mother proclaimed.

So the wedding went forward. But instead of a lavish sit-down formal wedding for 200, it was just a handful of close relatives and friends in Emily's parents' home.

Emily looked gorgeous in her white dress with puffy sleeves. But she didn't feel gorgeous. She felt sad, depressed, and confused. She was still absorbing the fact that her brother was dead and she would never get to see or speak to him again. There was so much more she needed to say to him—so many issues that remained unresolved. Emily remembered that her mother had ordered take-out fried chicken for everyone; a couple of photographs were taken; and the big day ended with Emily and her husband spending the night in the apartment they had been secretly sharing for months. They didn't even go to a hotel or take a honeymoon—an ominous way to start their marriage.

✦

ALL OF THESE MEMORIES HAD flooded back as Emily waited in the green room to be called for her segment. It felt like hours since she first arrived and met with the producer.

She looked around the room again and over at the table of food: doughnuts, coffee cake, bagels, cream cheese, jellies, preserves, grapes, and sliced cantaloupe. When she had first arrived, Emily had just glanced at the available foods. Now, she stood up and walked over to give it a much closer inspection. The donuts seemed to call out to her, "eat me." But she took a slice of cantaloupe instead and devoured it. However, then her stress began to mount and she grabbed half of a bagel. She smeared cream cheese on the bagel, piling it high, and then covered it with a thick layer of raspberry preserves. Emily pushed the bagel in her mouth, chewing in a furious way, putting all her stress and worry about her upcoming performance into every bite. The bagel worked like a drug. She couldn't even tell if it tasted good. It numbed her like Novocain. Despite the bagel, cream cheese and jam, the stress remained and she was still not being called to appear. So Emily grabbed a glazed doughnut. For a moment she toyed with the idea of putting the doughnut back and sitting down. She searched for other ways to soothe herself. But she didn't know what to do. Should she call Greg, who would be busy either getting the boys ready for school or on his way to work? She definitely didn't want to talk to her mother because she was afraid it might jinx her performance. She and her mother had a strained relationship, at best. Emily looked around the green room. There were other guests in the room but they were preoccupied with their own conversations. Everyone but Emily seemed to have brought one or more friends, family members, or their publicists along with them.

She pushed the glazed doughnut into her mouth. It tasted fresh and sticky but tasty as well. She had not had a doughnut in the longest time. Emily felt a satisfaction and a release that bordered on the sexual. It was almost as if she had come. How would she ever be able to explain it?

"You'll never guess what happened to me today—I was fucked by a glazed donut."

But it worked. The emptiness and tenseness in the deepest part of her psyche was temporarily sated. She sat down and stared somewhat blankly at the oversized TV screen hanging from the wall opposite the foods and beverages and smiled. Her reverie was broken when someone entered the room and announced ..."Emily Taylor. Follow me please."

Still in a bit of daze, Emily followed one of the studio crew out of the green room and down a hallway and into a well-lit set. She was seated on a sofa next to the morning show host.

Her mike was carefully placed on her right lapel. She took a deep breath to control her uneasiness, and allowed her excitement to take hold over what was about to unfold.

"In two ..." she heard someone say just a few feet from where she was sitting. And then, the lights grew brighter and ...

"Every day thousands are killed, ignored, or cheated on," Rosalie Brewster began, reading effortlessly from the teleprompter so no one outside the studio would know she wasn't speaking extemporaneously.

"Are we getting better or worse than ten years ago, even five years ago? What's happening today to help us feel connected to each other? To answer those questions I have psychotherapist and author, Dr. Emily Taylor, whose book, *Forgotten Intimacy*, has been on the bestseller list for the last six months. That's because Dr. Taylor has been touching a chord with so many of us. The study she reported on in her book jarred us with statistical truths that supported what we already knew anecdotally: we are in a moral quagmire and we need help getting out."

The camera switched to include Emily Taylor.

"Dr. Taylor, what are some of the greatest intimacy problems facing us today?"

"Too many lines are being crossed," Emily began.

"What lines, and why shouldn't they be crossed?"

"There are some lines that should not be crossed when it comes to actions or relationships, or the consequences could be dramatic, horrific, difficult to undo. Certain taboos exist because individuals and society need them to function."

"For example…"

"The taboo against murder. The taboo against cannibalism."

There was a short pause, on purpose, for emphasis.

"The taboo against extramarital affairs."

"Why is that such a dangerous line to cross?" Rosalie Brewster asked in that sparkling, energetic, and concerned tone that had made her the number one morning TV news co-anchor.

"Because such outside relationships usually diminish, destroy, or at least confuse and threaten the primary marital one. If there are problems in a marriage, sexual or emotional conflicts, most couples will do better to find solutions *within* their relationship. Other extramarital relationships cannot help their primary one; it is there where the energy and effort have to be put if a marriage needs help."

"So why are so many going *outside* for answers, not just in marriage but in other relationships, like friendships, letting the friendship go instead of 'doing the work,' as you so aptly put it in your book, *Forgotten Intimacy*, a good read, by the way?"

"The need for instant gratification has been fueled by our instant society," said Emily. "We have instant communication through e-mail, faster computers, and even higher speed limits on some highways so you can get to your destination faster without concern for the undeniable statistical correlation between a higher speed limit and more vehicle driving-related deaths."

Get back to the point, Emily told herself. Bring your audience back to your topic.

"So all these trends have to impact on how men and women, and peers, interact with each other."

"Of course," Rosalie Brewster replied, looking directly into Emily's eyes as their one-on-one conversation, shared with millions, reached its crescendo.

"Dr. Taylor, we think what you have to say is so important that we've asked our viewers to send in the questions about intimacy that they would most like answered. They have until three this afternoon to send their questions as e-mails to our web site. We'll read through all those responses and then, tomorrow morning, you and I will discuss your answers to the top ten questions that everyone wants you to address."

"I'll look forward to that," Dr. Taylor replied, completely confident and natural as if she had her own daily talk show.

The camera suddenly panned toward another part of the room as an assistant quickly removed Emily's microphone and rushed her off of the set before the next segment began.

"That was great," the producer said as she greeted Emily at the back of the studio, returning her pocketbook, which she had been holding for Emily through the interview. She just as quickly ushered Emily out of the studio.

"You were pleased?" asked Emily.

"Yes," the producer replied. "I think you got in all the points we discussed."

Yes, the interview had gone exceedingly well. Emily could tell. She had focused on communicating with the hostess and getting her ideas across, not on selling books or scoring points for witticisms. She also spoke in short "sound bites" and with the high energy that producers liked and audiences needed to keep them involved and awake.

Emily was glad that she got to say everything she had wanted to say. She tried to connect with the hostess but she knew that unless she returned, there was no reason for the hostess to connect with her. After all, she wasn't a celebrity. This hostess probably interviewed dozens, hundreds of people every year. How could she remember someone unless she or he was famous or there was a personal connection? Emily was neither.

EMILY ARRIVED AT HER SUBURBAN home, having caught a short nap in the car as it zoomed back against traffic. She used her keys to let herself in through the front door, instead of through the garage. One of her two cats, Cleo, greeted her. Emily immediately made her way to her office where she had a home phone and an office phone, each with voice mail.

"Hello, this is Beverly Granger," began the first message on Emily's voice mail, awaiting her return from the studio. "I don't know if you remember me but our sons went to preschool together. I saw you on *The Morning Show* today and you were fabulous. I didn't know you wrote a book on intimacy. I knew you were working on something but I didn't know you finished it and it was published. You were just so articulate and interesting. My number's in the telephone book and I know you're busy so don't worry about calling me back. I just wanted to say, congratulations."

"Hi, Emily. You were great! I'm so proud you're my girlfriend. Way to go, girl!" shouted one of Emily's best friends, Dale, from Delaware. Dale always knew the right thing to say and her timing was always impeccable. They had met while taking the same college course thirty years before and although they rarely saw each other more than once or twice a year, they always managed to be there for each other when it counted, emotionally or physically. Emily had already spoken with Greg before she left the studio as well as in the car, on the way home, on her cell phone. He thought she was terrific.

Still no phone message from her mother. She had hoped her mother's call would be the first.

"You were terrific," Dora, her sister, said, in message number three. "Very articulate. I'm proud of you."

"Great interview!" message four, Emily's editor.

"Emily, you were amazing!" Cousin Rachel, message five.

"I couldn't believe it when I turned on the TV this morning and there you were," message number six began. It was a former neighbor who had relocated to Florida. Emily hadn't heard from her in at least five years.

There were eight messages in total greeting Emily when she returned home. The house was empty, however. The boys were still in school and Greg was at work in Manhattan at the men's magazine where he was the Managing Editor. Everyone was where he was supposed to be.

Emily called her mother.

"I thought you'd have called by now," Emily began.

"You didn't give me a chance," Mrs. Keane replied. "I was going to call."

"Well?"

"You were terrific. And you looked beautiful."

"Thanks, Mom," Emily replied as she suddenly felt that sense of emptiness that so often flooded her entire being when she spoke to her mother. Was she hoping for an invitation to get together for a cup of coffee and chat about her appearance that morning? Her mother did not make the offer and Emily was not in a begging mood today.

THE NEXT MORNING, THE CAR arrived at 5:00 a.m. once again to drive Emily to *The Morning Show* for her second interview. This time she wore a lovely two-piece, floor-length yellow dress. The fabric was a delicate floral print with a silky look, a dramatic contrast to the austere navy blue business suit she had worn the day before.

The green room was once again set up with a sumptuous table of pastries, bagels, and coffeecakes, sliced fresh fruits, hard cheeses, and apples.

Emily eyed the spread and fondled one of the bagels. But this time, unlike the day before when she at least started with fruit, she grabbed a bagel, spreading globs of cream cheese on it, and topped it off with strawberry jam. She shoved half of it into her mouth, as if to devour as much of it as possible before anyone might notice her eating. She was pleased that the bagel was soft. This time she tasted it and it tasted better than she remembered a bagel could taste. For the next few minutes, Emily focused on eating her bagel, forgetting her fears about the questions she would be asked on this second day of follow-up questions about intimacy—Emily's answers to the most frequent questions selected from the 1,500 e-mails that her first interview had generated.

Emily was right. The hostess was friendlier on this second day. Two days in a row on *The Morning Show*. That was probably a first for anyone who was not either a celebrity or an employee.

Millions of people were watching Dr. Emily Taylor, commending what she said, how she looked, ordering her book, reading the sample chapter posted at the TV show's website.

So why was Emily feeling more uncomfortable than pleased by all this attention?

"Dr. Peters, where are you when I need you?" Emily thought, bemoaning the death the summer before of her psychological mentor and therapist of fourteen years. A man who had a gift for insight the way some artists have a magical ability to create astonishing paintings and some writers capture the imagination in plots, stories, or words that linger for a lifetime.

LATER THAT MORNING, EMILY FELT very uneasy when she was once again back in her empty house. The contrast between the excitement and activity of the TV show to the quiet and calm of her house seemed to heighten the anxiety that enveloped her like a strait-jacket. Although she had a lot of work to do, she felt distracted and unable to concentrate. She needed human contact, someone she could share her experiences with about the TV show this morning, someone face-to-face, not over the phone or through an e-mail communication on the Internet.

There weren't as many phone messages after the second interview but there were more than thirty e-mails for her to answer from men and women who had seen her on the shows, had visited her website, and now contacted her for personal responses to their intimacy questions. Emily had made a commitment to herself that she would answer each e-mail that she received, and she would. However, each e-mail had to be read, considered, and dealt with very carefully. Emily was very respectful of the time someone took to contact her, but for professional, legal, and personal reasons she could not dash off just any old answer to her newfound fans. And right now Emily needed someone to talk to, in person. It was simply too difficult to be alone after a second grand performance in front of millions. The disparity between the silence of her home, and the excitement, intensity, frenzy, and attention accorded to her over the previous two days caused Emily to suddenly experience a groundswell of isolation she had rarely felt in the last year.

Emily looked at her watch. She had to meet a client in another hour. At least she would be with someone, not just the silence of the house with Greg at work and the boys at school. But it would not be the same as having someone to chat with about her performances. It would be a client. She had to maintain her distance. Even sharing about her television appearances could be interpreted as unprofessional. What if it brought up jealousy feelings in her client and that became the focus of their session? No, her client had to lead the way in the session. Of course if she saw Emily on either of the shows, and her client was the first to bring it up, that would be different. But she doubted her client had seen either interview. Emily remembered that this particular client was usually at her office in Manhattan by eight each morning. She would have been commuting to work at the time that Emily was being interviewed. Maybe she set up her video recorder to tape it and she was going to replay it when she returned? An unlikely scenario. Besides, even if she had taped the show at home, her client probably did not have a chance to replay the tape before their session. Emily just had to accept the fact that her two interviews on national television were far more significant to her than to anyone else.

THE SESSION WITH HER CLIENT went well, considering how distracted Emily felt, and how tempted she was to say something about her morning talk show appearance. Afterwards, once she checked that she did not have any calls or e-mails that needed to be returned, she rushed back home.

Emily did not want to disturb Greg at the office so she decided to call Amanda at the weight loss center to seek her out for help. Emily had been going there for the last year and a half, following their reducing diet, as she managed to go from 210 to 135 pounds.

"I'd like to come in this morning," Emily said. "How late will you be there?"

"We'll be here for another hour."

"I'll be there in forty minutes."

Emily changed out of her dress into her favorite size 5 jeans. She put on running shoes, a tight tank top, and some fresh lipstick. It was only ten-thirty but it felt like it was later in the day. She had, after all, been up since four.

TRAFFIC WAS BRUTAL. There must have been an accident—the cars seemed to be at a standstill. The trip to the weight loss center that usually took just thirty minutes was taking more than an hour. Emily's cell phone was in her tote in the back of the car. Besides, she tried not to talk on the cell phone when driving. A part of her wanted to call Amanda and ask her to wait. Another part of her was confident that Amanda would be there to help her since she knew that Emily was on her way.

JUST ONE HOUR AND TEN MINUTES after she spoke to Amanda, Emily arrived at the weight loss center's office, breathless. She had run up the stairs after quickly parking her car as close to the center as possible.

Emily almost crashed through the front door as she tried to open it and rush in. But the harder she turned the handle on the front door, the more her hand hurt. The door knob was not moving.

"Amanda," Emily called out, banging on the front door. "It's Emily, Emily Taylor. Please open up."

All the way over, in the car, Emily had thought about all the things she wanted to share with Amanda: the rage she was feeling that she wanted so much to deal with in a non-food way. The emptiness she felt at having no one to share with about the amazing events of that morning. The public scrutiny that was so hard for Emily even though she knew it was important to expose herself this way for the sake of her book. Amanda was the one person Emily felt she could trust to be there for her. She had held it together until she got to the weight loss center. She was going to be able to vent and share with Amanda.

But Amanda was gone. Emily felt abandoned. Not even a

note on the front door. And Emily had only been ten minutes beyond the hour that Amanda said she was going to still be at the center. Just ten minutes. After more than a year, Amanda could not wait just ten more minutes for Emily?

Emily slumped down in front of the door as a sobbing started from her deepest being as it took over her, going from her feet all the way up through the top of her head. She reached into her pocketbook and took out the bag of chips that she had bought recently but had never gotten around to eating. She tore open the bag and started throwing chips into her mouth, first one at a time and then in fistfuls. Then she reached down further into her bag and retrieved a chocolate bar. Not just your average size one but an oversized bar that must have been more than 400 calories, filled with caramel. She bit into it, injecting it into her mouth, and swallowing the chocolate as if she were a drug-crazed addict.

"Amanda, how could you leave without even a note," Emily sniffed as she licked the rest of the chocolate from her fingers.

In a few seconds, her first real binge in a year, not counting the bagels and donuts in the green room, was over. She felt a mixture of relief and self-loathing. She knew that eating the potato chips and the chocolate bar had stopped her from plunging her fist through Amanda's door, which is what she really wanted to do. But then she felt nauseous from the food that she had consumed in such a short period of time. The rage and anxiety were soothed but she knew she would have to watch what she ate for the rest of the day, or at least work out for fifteen or thirty minutes, or she might start to show a weight gain from the added calories.

She had relied on Amanda and Amanda wasn't there for her. But the food. She could rely on food to be there, to help her out in her moments of despair. And even though there might be consequences and bit of weight gain, the food had come through for her. She was able to get through these horrendous feelings that were so debilitating that she almost had slight thoughts of suicide. The emptiness filled, those thoughts were gone now. She felt strangely calm, ready to go back out into the world, with or without Amanda's help.

Part Two

The Trip

OVER THE NEXT MONTH, Emily continued to work on her latest book, *The Return to Intimacy*, an extension of her intimacy studies, probing deeper into the roots of bonding and the long-term causes and consequences of dysfunctional family relationships (a topic about which she had first-hand experience). Meanwhile, her sons, Doug, fourteen, and Stan, ten, finished out their school year. She allowed them to spend the month of July just going to the swim club and taking it easy, rather than encouraging them to go to day camp or take courses, since she knew they were all planning to go away together during August.

With the boys now home from school, it was harder to concentrate on her work, as well as to stick to her weight control regimen. She had gained ten pounds since her appearance on *The Morning Show*; Emily could no longer zip up her favorite "thin" jeans, making it necessary to wear a pair that was not as form-fitting or flattering. She was starting to get concerned, but not fearful yet, since she was still a size 7. After all, she had kept off 60 pounds for more than a year now so it seemed reasonable she would get a grip soon and take off the ten she had regained, perhaps losing even more until she reached her goal weight of 132.

Yes, there was a return to some nervous eating but Emily still believed she had her eating under control, weighing and measuring each and every portion of fruit cup that she allowed herself, or each sandwich she might make with an ounce of hard cheese and three ounces of sliced turkey.

Emily fought the urge to binge on candy, ice cream or cake by consuming one, two, or even three cans of string beans with salsa. This had been her secret weapon in her battle to keep off the pounds.

Greg had agreed to take the boys and Emily on a business

trip to Europe since they were finally old enough to appreciate the experience.

"I don't know if I can handle the boys by myself," Emily confided to Greg. "Stan's still young. I'll be worried the whole time that he'll get lost and we'll be in a foreign country searching for him."

"I just thought you'd want to come along," Greg continued. "I know you've missed traveling all these years. This is a chance to get away as a family to Europe."

Emily and Greg went back and forth on the topic but it was clear that Emily wasn't going to give in. Her oldest son, Doug, was even willing to stay home with Emily's mother instead of going to Europe so Emily would only have to watch his younger brother.

But Emily didn't want to leave Doug behind—not after the abysmal time he had had the last time he spent a weekend with his grandmother. Nor did she want to be away from Doug for that length of time. She also wanted him to have this European vacation memory to reflect on forever, just as together, over the years, they had enjoyed watching the European family vacation movie starring Chevy Chase.

"Why don't we bring our babysitter along?" Emily asked. "I know a lot of families will bring a babysitter to the beach over the summer when they have young children. Why not bring her to Europe for two weeks?"

"Are you sure?" Greg asked. He knew what a private person Emily was; she liked visitors but she valued her alone time.

"It's the best solution, Greg."

"Fine," Greg said, somewhat reluctantly.

"Okay. I'll find out if she's able to come."

Their babysitter, Linda, had a fulltime job and babysat the boys twice a week for extra money and because she enjoyed spending time with them. Linda had wanted to be an elementary school teacher but she instead went into the family's real estate business.

Since Emily said she would pay for all her expenses including air fare, meals, and her own hotel room, Linda said she would love to go. Emily told the boys that they were going on a family trip at the end of August to London and Paris. They seemed much more excited that their babysitter Linda was coming along and that they did not have to go to summer camp this year.

Over the next week, Emily started to regret the whole idea. She had to tell her clients she would be in Europe during her August vacation. Because of the time difference, she strongly encouraged them to call the therapist covering for her if any emergency arose rather than trying to reach her. Emily would also be spending two weeks with Linda the babysitter and they had never been together for more than a few minutes. But backing out of her promise to take the boys to Europe was an unpleasant thought as well. Even Greg was looking forward to the family trip. So if she backed down now, she would be seen as someone whose word could not be respected, who broke promises and disappointed people. She flashed back on all the times her parents had made promises that they didn't keep without really good reasons for backing down, like the time her father said she could spend the summer of her freshman year at the University of Hawaii, only to change his mind. Emily still remembered how embarrassed she'd felt when she returned to college and everyone asked her about Hawaii and she had to say, "I didn't go."

She had made Doug, Stan, and Greg, and even Linda, a promise. She would go through with it. Besides, how bad could fourteen days be? Linda had always helped her oldest son to be more respectful toward Emily so she began to think having Linda along might make the trip a more positive experience. There would be plenty to do to keep everyone busy. She'd be with Greg and Doug and Stan; Linda was only coming along with them to help out when she was needed.

THE TRIP BEGAN WITH LINDA leaving her carry-on bag on the plane. Everything she held dear was in that backpack: portable CD player, CDs, reading material, $200 in spending money, and a wallet. (Fortunately, Emily was holding everyone's passports.) They spent at least an hour after arriving in Paris going from the airline's lost and found office to the cleaning crew to the airport's main lost and found room. Everything was very spread out and the end result was still the same: no sign of Linda's carry-on bag.

This isn't a good omen, Emily said to herself.

After recovering from jet lag, the next two days went quite well for the four Taylors and their babysitter. Traveling together was a novelty to everyone; they were still marveling at how this trip that they had been planning and looking forward to for weeks had finally arrived.

They toured Paris—the Eiffel Tower, the Louvre Museum, walking along the Champs Elysées. Greg had a business meeting every now and then, and Emily left the boys with Linda so she could make a quick trip to her French publisher's offices.

Then they took the Chunnel train from Paris to London, traveling under the English Channel for a short portion of the four-hour ride. When they checked into their London hotel, Emily was impressed by their plush accommodations. Greg's company was picking up the tab for their room so they only had to pay for the separate room for the boys and another room for Linda. It was one of the few hotels in London to have an indoor pool, although they were told upon checking in that the pool was having its annual maintenance. It would be closed during their stay.

But by the third day, Emily was longing for the privacy of spending time with just her own family. Why didn't all her psychological wisdom help her to predict that Doug, Stan, and Linda would become a little subgroup, shutting out her and Greg? When Greg was involved with a business appointment, it increased Emily's anxious and lonely feelings since Linda and the boys all seemed to be bonded together. Stan, her younger son, instead of wanting to spend time with his mother, preferred to be with Linda and Doug even when Emily asked Stan to do something with just her.

By the fourth day of their trip, Emily, who already had become less strict about what she ate, began slipping even more. At the "all you can eat" breakfasts, she added an extra starch or two, a roll with butter and jam, several strips of bacon, hard cheese, and two portions of scrambled eggs and hash brown potatoes.

By the fifth day, she was adding oatmeal to the enormous breakfast as well as hard candies and chocolates throughout the day to help her get through it. Each day felt three times as long as normal and she wondered how she would ever get through nine more days.

They were leaving the new Tate Gallery in London, a renovated old Railroad Station that made such a commanding impression that it was harder to focus on the contemporary art that it housed, when Greg pulled Emily aside.

"Darling, I've noticed you're eating more," Greg said in a caring, nonjudgmental tone.

"I know. Don't worry about it. I'm fine."

"But you've been doing so well," Greg continued. He had seen Emily's weight go up and down for the last sixteen years and although he was fine with her appearance, regardless of her weight, he knew that it upset Emily when she was overweight.

"I've got things under control," Emily said.

"So what's going on?"

"I'm just a little tense about the trip," Emily explained. "And I miss writing. You know how important it is for me to keep working everyday and I can't write on the trip."

"Why not? You brought your laptop. Why don't you use it?" Greg asked.

"I just can't," Emily replied. "I want to write but I can't concentrate. And I feel I should be out and about with Linda and the boys, touring, soaking up the sights."

"But it was your idea to have her come along," Greg reminded her.

"I know. And I'm glad she's here. We're here. I'm just struggling with the lack of routine."

Emily couldn't believe she was using the word *routine*. To most outsiders, since she worked from home most of the time, unless she was conducting on-site interviews, seeing clients, doing seminars, or consulting, Emily's workday seemed to lack a routine. After all, her day did not have the structure of the traditional nine-to-fiver. But Emily actually had a very strict routine. She was at her computer by five each morning, enabling her to get at least an hour of work in before the family awakened. If she didn't get too immersed in her work, or checking her e-mails, she made breakfast for the boys and then headed back to work after Greg and the boys left for the day.

At noon, if she was still home, she took her lunchtime break, watching the mid-day news. As soon as it was over, it was back to work until she met the school bus. Or, if she had paperwork to do, she would stop her creative work at two and turn on the two o'clock movie on *Lifetime*, having it in the background while she typed cover letters or put together mailings.

If she had to do an interview as research for a new writing project, conduct a seminar, or see a client, her day was completely different. Her writing would be put on hold for that day, or done in the early evening, while the boys were supposed to be doing their homework and Greg was either doing additional copyediting or writing for the magazine that employed him. She rented outside office space for seeing clients on an hourly basis. Since she had reduced her client load when the boys were born, short-term renting was more economical than leasing monthly space at the medical center. She only saw five clients a week, at the most. Before the boys were born, she was seeing as many as five to ten clients a day, as well as conducting two or three evening group therapy sessions.

Therefore, to Emily, there was a clear routine to her weekdays. And even though she longed to be around her peers, she knew that this was the best set-up for her now.

LATER THAT DAY, LINDA WENT SHOPPING, and Greg took the boys on a tour of London—to the Tower of London, Big Ben, and various other well-known historical spots—while Emily met her British publisher, John Miller, for an early dinner. He was an odd-looking fellow, with thick reddish hair that hung over his forehead like a poor-fitting toupee. He was in his early sixties and had been in the book business since he graduated from Oxford University with a degree in English. He had entered publishing when it was still considered a "gentleman's profession" and had witnessed its change to big business just in the last decade, a full twenty years after the changeover was completed in the States.

For his entire adult life, even beginning during his private prep school years, everyone assumed John was gay since he lived with his elderly mother in a tiny three-story house on the outskirts of London. But five years before, John surprised his colleagues when, within days of his mother's funeral, he moved in with a girlfriend whom he told everyone he was engaged to marry. In time, everyone stopped asking him when the wedding was going to be; behind his back, they referred to John and his girlfriend as the engaged couple who lived together and would probably never actually marry.

"I've been able to set up an interview for you on the top morning BBC show while you're here," John said over dinner.

Emily thanked the waiter for bringing a second bread tray.

"Great. The BBC. I'm thrilled about that."

There was an awkward silence and then Emily asked, "How are sales?"

"*Forgotten Intimacy* doesn't seem to be doing as well here as it's been doing in the States, but I'm confident sales will pick up."

"Any radio interviews set up during my trip?" Emily asked.

"Not yet. But I've got at least one newspaper reporter from one of the two major dailies interested in interviewing you tomorrow morning, plus a freelance journalist who thinks he can sell a story about you to one of the most popular monthly magazines."

"Sounds good," Emily continued as she poured ranch dressing all over her salad.

"So what are you working on now?" John asked.

Emily was jarred by his question. She instantly regretted her decision not to keep working on her new book so she could brag about her progress. Initially, she welcomed the idea of a two-week break from writing but now she missed it. Having an occasional business appointment or interview seemed like enough time away from the boys and Greg on the trip. If she got consumed in her writing, as she always did when she was creating and not just doing busywork, would have meant too much time apart—mentally as well as physically. She had finally managed to put the new book out of her mind until John's question.

"We'd like to see it, of course. I believe we have an option on it. What's it about?"

"I prefer not to talk about my work in progress," Emily explained, trying not to offend John by withholding details about her new work. "It somehow dissipates the energy that I need to actually take a book from idea to completion if I talk about it. But I can tell you that it's a follow-up to *Forgotten Intimacy*. It takes those basic concepts and explores them in an amazing way."

"I know what you mean," John said. "Most of my authors feel that way. Especially the novelists."

They switched to discussing other topics until their main courses arrived.

"Seen any good plays lately?" Emily asked as she took another forkful of mashed potatoes.

"*Stones in His Pocket* is quite good."

"We're planning to see that tonight."

"I don't get out to the theatre as much as I used to."

"It's become more like Broadway here than I remembered it to be. I mean price-wise. Theatre tickets aren't that much of a bargain anymore."

"London is much more expensive than Manhattan right now," John agreed. "Not just for theatre tickets but for hotels and restaurants as well."

"I've noticed."

"What's your husband doing now with your children?"

"I'm not sure. I think they were going to one of the arcades at Piccadilly Circus. Maybe they went to a castle or a movie. We're meeting up at the theatre later."

The waiter came by with a dessert cart with cheesecakes swimming in sauce, apple pie, chocolate custard pie, raspberry tarts, seven-layer chocolate cake, and mousse topped with fresh whipped cream.

"No, thank you," Emily said.

"Come on, Emily," John pleaded. "The seven-layer chocolate cake is my favorite. And you obviously don't have to worry about what you eat."

Emily was flattered.

"Thank you for saying that, but I do."

"But you are so slim compared to when we first met," John remarked, almost blushing when he realized he was probably speaking much too intimately to an author and business associate.

"Thank you for noticing. Well, I guess this one time it can't do that much harm."

"The lady will have a piece of your chocolate cake," he instructed the waiter. "Nothing for me," he added.

After dinner, Emily got into a cab and headed back to the hotel to rest and freshen up before meeting Greg, Linda, and the boys. She was tired but, as she almost always did when she entered into a hotel room in a strange city, she turned on the television. It was more like background noise than serious watching; just something to fill the silence.

In the hotel room was a mini-bar, stocked with chocolate bars, pretzels, popcorn, miniature alcoholic drinks, soft drinks, juice, water, and nuts. She took out a chocolate bar and a bag of salted peanuts and started to devour the chocolate bar as she waited alone in the hotel room as if time had ceased.

Eating, and overeating, seemed the only way that Emily could find to soothe herself. She had made a mistake by going on this trip and she was paying for it. The boys and Greg were doing fine with Linda along. Sure, Greg would like it to be just the family, but he could get through the rest of the trip. They just agreed never to do this again and for Greg that was enough to help him through London and their next stop, Amsterdam, with their babysitter Linda in tow. Besides, Greg had business appointments in each city, lasting several hours in the middle of the day, so it was Emily who had to spend even more time alone or with the boys and Linda. Having Linda to talk to and to help out with childcare still seemed like a good idea but it was an idea that was not working as smoothly as Emily had hoped it would.

They had separate rooms from the boys and Linda and, because they now numbered five they had to take two taxis instead of one whenever they went anywhere. Linda and the boys took one and she and Greg, the other. Dividing the family like this upset Emily more than she wanted to admit.

MEANWHILE, THE OVEREATING continued non-stop, even though Emily kept reassuring herself that she could stop it once she was back home. (Besides, how much weight could she possibly gain in just two weeks after taking off 77 pounds and keeping 67 pounds off for more than a year?)

The trip was beginning to bring up thoughts from her past that she hadn't known were still bothering her. Emily's initial response was to try to avoid them and to soothe herself by consuming food. The memories were not something she dwelt on consciously. There was just something about having an outsider along on the trip that had triggered the uncomfortable feelings she had always attached to a secret—and forbidden—relationship from her childhood.

Was she naïve not to think that such feelings would be brought up by spending so many hours for so many days with this attractive young woman, half her age? She trusted Greg and was not at all jealous of Linda but she wondered if it was too much closeness for Doug and Stan with their babysitter. Emily now realized she was a fool to have put herself in this position. She knew she would never do this again. Now she just had to get through it, get through the next week, as best she could.

ONE OF THE REASONS THAT her mother went to work full-time when Emily was ten was that she could not stand being in the house when Dolores, the maid, was there. Before she worked full-time, Emily's mother filled her days by being out of the house shopping, or being dragged by her wealthier friend Carol to luncheons that she found very boring.

"Why didn't you like being in the house when Dolores was there?" Emily had finally asked her mother.

"I didn't like watching Dolores do all the work."

"The work?"

"Yes, the housework."

"But, Mother," Emily responded, incredulously. "She was our maid. That's what you paid her to do. To do the housework."

Emily was baffled by her mother's response but decided to probe her further.

"Okay, so you didn't like to watch Dolores 'do the work.' So why didn't you fire her?"

"Oh, no. Dolores was like one of the family. That would have been like getting rid of my own child."

TO EMILY, BEING WITH Linda for two weeks in Europe was like having Dolores in the house when she was growing up: she felt ambivalent about her presence because Dolores was not really a family member. She was an intruder who enabled her mother to avoid interacting with Emily, just as Linda gave Emily's older son Doug an excuse to avoid her and Doug's younger brother Stan for most of the trip.

Stan, a quiet and amenable child, worshipped his older brother and would never complain about Doug and the babysitter. But Emily began to notice that Stan was becoming even quieter than usual and reticent to the point of almost seeming mute.

Eventually she confronted Linda. "You and Doug have to make Stan feel more included."

"I'll try, Dr. Taylor," Linda dutifully replied.

"But we *do* include Stan!" Doug shouted.

Emily realized that, in theory, Doug was right. The three of them were all doing activities together, like going on rides at the amusement park while Emily and Greg sat at a table, watching the crowds, sipping the local beer. How could she demand that Stan, a full four years younger, be included in every conversation between Doug and Linda?

But whenever Linda or Emily asked the boys to clean up the clothes strewn around their hotel room, Doug managed to get Stan to do the work for both of them, and that annoyed Emily and Linda.

"Stan, what are you doing here?" Emily asked Stan when she found him in the hotel lobby early one morning.

"Doug asked me to get him something to eat. He didn't want to wait for breakfast."

"Stan, you're not supposed to be walking around the hotel by yourself!" Emily explained. "And just because Doug asks you to do something, doesn't mean you have to say 'yes.' You don't have to do everything your brother asks you to do," she continued.

Consciously, what mattered to Emily was that nothing bad happened on the trip. On the surface, it was a successful trip and the experiment of having their babysitter Linda along seemed to work out just fine. Greg even said that having Linda along was "no big deal" for him.

But for Emily, getting through those two weeks was fast becoming excruciating as the deep-seated feelings being stirred up were compounded by Stan's submissiveness, Doug's exclusive chumminess with his babysitter, and Linda's often ignoring her. Yet Emily was unable to confront Linda about this behavior since Linda, ostensibly, was not doing anything wrong. But each day seemed like a week, and overeating was the way that Emily eased herself through.

She did much of her overeating at the hotel buffet breakfasts, which in her mind meant that once the trip was over and she was back at home, her breakfast-eating would return to normal.

LOOKING BACK AT THE European trip, Emily also discovered something else: she really did feel comfortable with her own family, a feeling she had never known as a child or teen. She could see a distinct difference in how she felt when it was just she and the boys, or she and Greg and the boys, versus having Linda along. The uneasy way she felt during those fourteen days in Europe was closer to the unsettled way she felt in her own home for the sixteen years she lived there before going away to college. But it was behind her now.

They were back home in New Jersey. She had finally returned to her safe and comfortable surroundings with their two cats, Hercules and Cleo, her own pillow with just the right amount of softness, and the birds chirping when she awoke to get some quiet writing time in before everyone else awakened. Doug and Stan would be starting school again in just a few days. Greg had returned to his commuter routine. Yes, Emily had her familiar life back and all would be the way it was before they went away on that exciting but unnerving trip.

Part Three

The Pretty One

*I*T STARTED SO INSIDIOUSLY. Emily had allowed herself a few days after returning from the trip to adjust and wind down from the pressure and the stress. She was confident she would be able to get back on the wagon, controlling what she ate, and when she ate, the way she had been doing for the last year-and-a-half before her first slip in the green room of *The Morning Show*. That same prevailing vigilance and commitment would make her successful at her weight loss and maintenance this time. Emily was confident that she had licked her compulsive overeating problem. She would be back on track in a few more days at the most. She had only gained ten pounds on the trip, and even though that added up to 20 pounds since her appearance on *The Morning Show*, she had still kept off more than 40. She was determined not to backslide further.

This time she was going to lose the twenty she gained, and then go back to meeting her goal of 132.

This was just a temporary relapse. It wasn't even a relapse. Just a setback because of the trip.

She could control it. She wasn't going to keep eating and overeating to soothe the rage with food.

But there it was, two weeks after she returned home from Europe—back with a vengeance. The obsession, the compulsive eating, the bingeing. The addiction to certain foods.

Did she have "a problem" or was she just "overeating?" Emily checked her reference materials hoping to put her problem into the proper perspective. Did she have binge-eating disorder, first specified in 1992 to distinguish it from the two other primary eating disorders: anorexia nervosa (refusing to eat, sometimes to the point of starvation) and bulimia nervosa (bingeing, followed by purging or regurgitating)? Or obesity (having a body mass index [BMI] of 30 or higher, or weighing 30 or more pounds more than the recommended weight range for that individual's height, weight, and activity level)?

Why can't I stop myself? Emily pleaded.

Every morning, each afternoon, and every night, she said, yet again, "Just today. I have to get through today and then I'll start watching what I eat," or, "I'll go back on a diet tomorrow."

She was grabbing this and grabbing that, and it all went into her mouth—mostly when no one else was looking. Even the portions she ate at each meal had gotten bigger. They were just a little more at first, but soon became almost twice what she was supposed to eat to keep herself from gaining more weight.

ANOTHER WEEK WENT BY and Emily was still compulsively over-eating and bingeing. It had started so simply—losing control over that bagel with cream cheese and jelly in the green room at *The Morning Show*—and it had escalated and continued over the weeks and now months that followed.

She simply allowed her impulse to be acted out rather than controlled. From that one action, that one bagel, so much havoc had been wrought, so much weight had been gained, and so much self-esteem had been compromised.

Emily tried to take her attention away from food and bingeing and to put that energy, that focus, into working on her new book, *The Return to Intimacy*, the follow-up to her bestseller, *Forgotten Intimacy*. She had a good working relationship with her editor and wanted to make her deadline but ever since the trip, it had been hard for Emily to force herself to interview others about their intimacy problems and triumphs. Yet conducting interviews, and doing research, were two of the tasks of discovery related to writing nonfiction that Emily usually enjoyed.

The combination of the trip and the topic of her new book had revived her own feelings and conflicts about intimacy even more. So many of the men and women she interviewed for this new book assured Emily that the process of being interviewed was cathartic for them. Or they'd say, "I really needed to share this with someone. It was keeping me up at night." She needed to share her feelings with someone—and soon.

There was something about her exposure on national television followed by the trip to Europe that had catapulted Emily into a deep depression. And overeating was how she coped with the flood of overwhelming emotions. She found herself being pulled back into her deepest secrets and her worst memories. She turned to food to comfort the painful feelings and horrendous memories curdling to the surface.

She was no longer a successful fifty-year-old author, psychologist, wife, and mother but a frightened, sad, fearful ten-year-old. For that was when Emily's childhood ended. It was then that her beloved older brother Martin, who was thirteen, the one she looked up to, the one she idolized, had begun to sexually abuse her. He would continue the abuse intermittently over the next nine years. Each of the molestations ended with her brother crying and begging, "Don't tell!"

Another important event occurred during that fateful tenth year—Emily got her period for the first time. Her mother didn't provide a very thorough explanation of what it meant. Her sister Dora would not get her period for another three years, so she was not much help. Emily remembered her mother telling her at the time, "You can get pregnant now so don't let a boy touch you." When Emily's boyfriend at sleep-away camp kissed her that summer, she spent the rest of the summer worrying that she might be pregnant.

Her mother's pronouncements also made what was happening with her brother that much more frightening. If being touched could make her pregnant, what was going to happen from the things her brother was asking her to do to him?

It began on a day in the spring when she and her brother were alone in the house. Dolores the housekeeper had gone to the store, and Dora was visiting a friend. It was after school and Emily was in her bedroom, sitting at her desk reading Salinger's *Nine Stories* when Martin entered and closed the door behind him, then locked it. He then turned off the overhead light, making the room darker, with late afternoon sunlight providing the only illumination.

"Hey," cried Emily. "Why did you do that?"

"Shhhh," replied Martin. He walked over to her, staring at her chest. Although Emily was only ten, she had started to develop breasts and they were pushing against the white cotton blouse she wore. Martin reached out and unbuttoned the top two buttons and then let his hand slide beneath the blouse. He cupped her right breast in the palm of his hand, holding it gently at first and then softly squeezing until he could feel her nipple harden under his touch. A chill of excitement and fear ran through Emily's body. She immediately became confused over how good it felt and how wrong she knew this was.

"Martin," she said, "what are you doing?"

"Does that feel good?" asked Martin, looking down at her with an intense, loving expression that made her feel wanted and desired in a way she had never known before.

"Yes," admitted Emily, still regaining her equilibrium from the lightheadedness over having her breasts touched.

Before she could continue Martin slid his right hand over her left breast and Emily let out a moan.

"Now touch me," said Martin.

"Martin, I ...."

"Down here," and he guided Emily's now trembling hand to his already hard penis pushing against his pants. Emily could feel it throbbing, trying to burst through the fabric. Martin unzipped his pants and his penis sprung free through the opening. He pushed her hand around it. She didn't know what to do next, so he showed her by moving her hand up and down the shaft, with his hand on top of hers, guiding it as he moved it up and down, faster and faster.

Emily closed her eyes in fear. Her mother's voice echoed in her mind: "You can get pregnant now, just by touching a boy." She tried to distance herself from the action, as if she were observing someone else in the midst of this drama. She made a face indicating displeasure but she was turned away from Martin so he couldn't see how what he was doing was impacting his little sister. Not that it would have made any difference because when she finally opened her eyes and looked at him, he was in intense ecstasy, completely involved in the sexual sensations he was feeling, almost as if he were in a trance.

Emily felt queasy when Martin came, and his cum squirted all over her hands, blouse, floor and desk. It seemed to get everywhere and all Emily could think was how she was going to explain the mess to her sister who shared the bedroom with her.

ONCE IT BEGAN, WHENEVER SHE and Martin were alone in the house, he would come to her bedroom and repeat the scene. But after a while and many messes later, Martin introduced Emily to a new form of gratification. Instead of pushing her hand toward his penis, he pushed her head down. She struggled at first, but he overpowered her and she gave in. At first, he pushed down so hard she gagged. His penis was too big for her small throat and she was afraid she was going to choke. She kept her eyes closed tight during the entire experience. This didn't feel as good as when the abuse had begun and when she had actually felt pleasure over having her breasts fondled. This was hard work and she especially hated swallowing his ejaculation. But she looked up to her brother. She trusted him. She didn't want to get him in trouble and she was afraid to tell her parents. They put Martin on a pedestal and rarely said "no" to him. What if her parents didn't believe her? It would be her word against his. More importantly, what if Martin stopped doing what he was doing and ignored her the way she felt everyone else was ignoring her?

UNFORTUNATELY, EMILY DID not feel she could trust anyone with her secret. She did not believe there was anyone within her family or any teacher or family friend to whom she could turn for help. At that time, it was less widespread to have sex education or child sexual abuse teaching aids to tell children how to say "no," especially to family members—including an older brother.

She was still angry about it and anger was an emotion she never handled very well. As a child, she would have unexplained temper tantrums, sometimes throwing a book or a chair against her bedroom wall. She would not allow herself to be angry at her brother for some inexplicable reason, so she turned the anger inward, and started to hate herself for being unable to say "no" to him. She hated her parents for not protecting her from what she was experiencing.

"Why did you pick me and not my sister?" Emily remembered asking her brother.

"Because you're the pretty one," he replied as he stroked her cheek and brown hair.

All her life, being considered "pretty" had haunted her. What should have been a positive trait had turned into a negative connotation because of the sexual abuse she experienced. Often, whenever people tried to distinguish Emily from her sister who was only two years older, they would say, "Dora is the smart one" and "Emily is the pretty one."

Over time, a strange thing began to happen. Despite the negative feelings she had about what her brother was doing to her, Emily began to integrate her brother's intermittent sexual abuse into her life. She even started to look forward to when it would next happen, and what would happen. She was curious about the sensations he was evoking in her, and the power she had over Martin. She was not concerned enough with whether it was right or wrong, or how it might be destroying what should have been her carefree, non-sexual, preadolescent years.

The time the sexual abuse began was the same point that Emily began to struggle with weight, a fight that would become a lifelong problem. At ten, she wasn't obese, just five or ten pounds overweight. But when you're a little girl, and you feel chubby and unattractive, that's a lot of pounds. The real weight gain began soon after she did a seductive dance in leotards and a tank top before 200 guests at her brother's Bar Mitzvah. No one seemed to think anything about it, or asked her what was bothering her or why.

Also when she was ten, the year the sexual abuse began, Emily wrote a 225-page novel, typing every page herself. But no one noticed, let alone read it.

✦

UNFORTUNATELY, SHE LOST THAT novel although she did keep a copy of a full-length play that she wrote when she was thirteen. It was called *La Familia*. Its story unfolded from a younger sister's point-of-view. It was about an older brother who falls down the stairs on the way to breakfast and breaks his leg. He has to go to the hospital to have his leg set in a cast. He falls in love with the nurse. Then it's a boy-loses-girl, boy-wins-back-girl scenario.

The only person she ever showed the play to was her father. He never said anything about it and that devastated her. She felt rejected. She couldn't believe her father had simply ignored this incredible achievement—a full-length play at the age of thirteen. She figured she couldn't write fiction and it would be years before she would try again to write a full-length play or a novel.

When she was 33, Emily finally got up the courage to ask her father about that incident with the play. He said, "I didn't say anything because I didn't think it was that good." She remembered how she started crying as she replied, "But Daddy. I was thirteen years old. How bad could it have been?"

Then her father shared the real reason he hadn't said anything. "I wanted you to become a chemist, or something *secure*. Writing would be such a hard life. I wanted you to do something else. You were so smart and you were good in science. You could have been anything you wanted."

Emily realized that in a way, her father's approach had worked; she had become a psychologist and not "just" a writer.

Her father had also tried to influence her brother to become a doctor. In those days, as now, there was high status attached to being able to say, "My son, the doctor." A doctor's economic future seemed ensured. Like Emily, her brother felt his creativity did not receive the parental encouragement it deserved.

It was her brother who praised Emily's creative efforts. He gave her the attention she felt was lacking from her parents or her sister. He also was her literary mentor, recommending books she might enjoy. At eleven she was reading Tolstoy's *War and Peace* and Ibsen's *The Wild Duck*.

Looking back now, Emily wished she had had the emotional courage to confront her parents about their neglect. She wished she could have told her sister how much it hurt to be left out whenever she went away with their cousin and her family on trips to Vermont or to the Poconos. How painful it was when they visited on Sundays and her sister and her cousin locked her out of their cousin's room because their cousin said she was too young to play with them. It was definitely tough to be two years younger than her sister. "The baby." Of course, her sister had a right to her own friends, whatever their ages, but Emily and Dora were close enough in age that they could have shared some friends or certainly their cousins. Emily just suffered in silence.

One of her favorite positive childhood memories was the 36-inch mosaic tile table that the family created. There was a big "K" in the middle of the table surrounded by rings of turquoise and gold tiles. In her diary, which she began keeping when she was ten, she wrote:

We are almost finished with the table. It is so beautiful and I mean it.

And when it was finally finished a few days later, she added:

Table was finished. It is so beautiful. Everyone in the family helped make it. It took only 3 days to make the table.

How she wished she had more childhood memories of doing positive activities together as a family to relate to as she raised her own children.

Ironically, when Emily was ten years old and the sexual abuse began, she was considered one of the most popular girls in class. She was sure some of her popularity was her reputation for giving terrific slumber parties and co-ed parties. She also put a lot of time and energy into working with other students when they were put on committees to do collaborative reports. The popularity was more like that of a politician. Other than one girlfriend at school, Sandy, whom she never saw outside of school, and her next-door neighbor, Sally, Emily did not feel connected to anyone, certainly not to her mother.

Emily had a very involved sixth grade class that year and a superbly caring, dedicated, hardworking teacher named Mrs. Small. (How she now wished she had trusted Mrs. Small enough to go to her for help!) Her classroom was also the music room for the school, filled with drums and other instruments. Emily liked being surrounded by music. Mrs. Small would always have an opera or a classical piece of Beethoven, Bach, or Brahms playing in the background.

That year they did a school musical. Everyone thought Emily should get the lead but someone else with a better voice was chosen instead. She could still remember the words to the songs. It was a take-off on *South Pacific* but it was about New Jersey instead.

Emily did get the lead in the class dramatic play, however. She played a judge. The only performance was during the school day and her mother felt she couldn't get away from her administrative job to see her. Emily's father, a doctor with more flexible hours, came instead. She was crushed that her mother wasn't there. A few years later, Emily's mother apologized for not going to the play.

"I had just started my job. I just couldn't have taken time off to see you," she said. "Maybe if it had been ten years later."

Emily felt sorry for her mother when she confided that. But then she thought to herself: ten years later! Emily would have been twenty by then and already married for the first time. It was when she was ten that she needed her mother to be there for her. Emily was too young to understand how a working mother sometimes has to make hard choices.

But Emily performed well in school so no one thought she was having problems at home. She was always a good student ranging from A to B. Someone would have had to notice the changes in Emily's self-esteem, or body image, or notice that she rarely seemed to be feeling happy, or joyful, in order to speculate about how Emily was doing emotionally.

Emily wondered if she'd gone along with the sexual abuse and didn't tell her parents because she had been to sleep-away camp at the age of five for eight weeks. Maybe in her child's mind, she feared that if she told them, they would send her away again—and for longer or forever. She now realized she had already shut down emotionally by the time she was five, and was reluctantly shipped off to summer camp for eight weeks with just one day for parents to visit between the first and second months.

Emily also now considered that if she was unable to tell her parents she hated summer camp and wanted to come home, how was she going to tell them something far worse—that their only son, her "perfect" brother was sexually abusing her?

Emily grew up feeling unsafe in her own home, with the scars always there, even if she no longer remembered the details of the events. There was that hot coffee cup that Emily reached up to grab, or so the story goes, when she was still in a high chair, toppling it on her shoulder, causing a third degree burn that left a lifelong scar, far more prominent in her early years. Another time, she was running around the house while her parents were entertaining, chasing her sister Dora, falling and getting a huge gash in her face that her father sutured himself, leaving another lifelong scar on her forehead. This one was harder to hide than her shoulder scar since it was on her face.

AT TEN, EMILY WAS petrified by the situation with Martin. The consequences of telling seemed to outweigh the benefits of silence so that she shut down emotionally even further than when she was sent to camp.

In addition to being angry that her brother put her in this untenable position, she also felt guilty about her part in it. She now realized that she dealt with her guilt by blaming her mother for what was happening as well as for failing to be the kind of mother to whom she could confess anything. But since she never told her, Emily had allowed her fear of what her mother might do to prevent her from even giving her mother a chance to react. Emily's fear was all-consuming, and so debilitating that she was willing to endure years of abuse instead of confronting her own mother.

Her brother used emotional coercion to continue his inappropriate sexual behavior with Emily over the next nine years. But it was not reciprocal. Because of that, at an early age, Emily learned a negative lesson about sex—that girls give sexual pleasure to boys. It would be a long time before she would also learn, through appropriate sexual relationships, and therapy, and her training for her Ph.D. in psychology, that girls could *get* pleasure as well as give it. It would take decades for her to find a man who could restore the trust that her brother had taken from her.

Emily was sure that was why it had taken a lot of time, effort, and therapy for her to learn to relate in a mature, equal, and non-abusive way to other authority figures or to a romantic partner. To be able to stand up for her rights and feelings, and to be able to disagree without thinking the world would fall apart, had been huge steps for her.

It was simple now for Emily to belittle herself, blame herself, and to ask: "Why didn't I say, 'No?'"

How convenient for Emily to harshly judge herself, because she now felt loved. She developed the inner strength about her ability to stand on her own, and she learned that liking herself was more important than anyone else's approval, even her parents' or her brother's. But then, when she was ten, she felt alone and adrift. Her brother's attention, albeit it wrong, offered her a life raft. She was afraid to turn him down. If she pushed her brother away, and her parents and sister weren't there for her, the thought of being all alone emotionally was scarier than doing what her brother asked her to do.

What amazed her the most about those nine years of sexual abuse was that no one suspected anything, and she had never wavered in her agreement not to tell.

AROUND THE TIME THE abuse began, Emily remembered her mother saying something to her about an acquaintance of hers whose son happened to be in Emily's sixth grade class. She said that the mother was unwilling to leave her two children, a brother and his sister, home together without an adult present because she was afraid they might do something with each other. Emily didn't remember if her mother used the word *sexual* or simply implied it, but she still remembered how she froze when her mother said it.

THE NEXT YEAR, HER FATHER defied her mother by making a decision, and a really big one, entirely on his own. On the way back from a fishing trip with her brother, he decided to go house-hunting, and bought a weekend house for $27,000 in a little town near the Jersey shore. They would begin spending occasional winter weekends and the entire summers at that house—which was almost as big as their New Jersey home and could be used all year round—for the next two years.

Those two years taught Emily an incredible lesson: what children find wonderful and exciting can be awful and unpleasant for their parents. So her mother, who had her routine and her ways of avoiding her children at their house, was stuck in the sticks with them for the entire summer. They were dependent on her for transportation whereas in Maplewood, even by the age of ten, Emily and her twelve-year-old sister had started taking the town bus that stopped on the corner. They would take it to the train station and then take the train or the bus to the department store in Newark or even in Manhattan, followed by a double feature at the movies, and getting something to eat at a coffee shop. Sometimes they would get Saturday matinee standing-room-only tickets for just ten or twenty dollars to a hit Broadway show.

So the summer home that Emily loved because they were outside all day swimming, boating, and exploring nature and the woods without the restrictions and supervision of camp was experienced as awful by her mother. Her mother hated it there.

At that time, her mother was a coffee drinker and a heavy chain smoker. From Friday night until Saturday night, her mother did not have a cigarette. It was somehow tied to it being the Sabbath, the Jewish day of rest, as well as a promise she made to herself when her father died. Anyone who's ever quit smoking knows how torturous those first twenty-four hours are; her mother did that to herself, every single week. She would get moodier, more short-tempered, and more critical of Emily than usual. Then, as night began to fall on Saturday, she would allow herself to again light up, and become more herself.

It was harder for her mother to hide from her children those two summers at Crystal Lake, but she still managed. Especially during the week, since Dolores the cleaning lady was always there to attend to their basic food and clothing needs. Emily had no memories of her mother during those two summers except the one time she took all three children to a recreated colonial village. Her memories of those summers were of she, and her sister, and their local friends. Her brother was off with his older friends. Emily didn't remember seeing him too much during those summers, either, except for the time he had some *shav* (Jewish spinach soup) from the local supermarket and he found it tasted awful. He asked her to taste it to see if he was right. Like a fool, she tasted it and agreed it was rancid. But they both got food poisoning and had to have their stomachs pumped out at a Catholic hospital a few miles away.

She had so much faith in her brother (unfortunately too much blind faith) that she did whatever he asked. Like tasting contaminated soup.

IT WAS HARD TO KNOW WHAT was going on in her brother's head when the abuse began since he died when he was twenty-three and he did not keep a diary. She gathered together whatever letters or compositions that Martin had saved that might give some clues. All that Emily could figure out was that her brother was very insecure, especially about his appearance, considering himself too short (he was only 5 foot 8 inches). He obviously did not see himself in the same way that everyone else did, especially his parents, male peers, and professors, who thought he was talented, energetic, handsome, and innovative.

✦

THE DEADLINE FOR HER new book, *The Return to Intimacy*, was looming as Emily tried to focus on transcribing interviews and finishing up the first complete draft of the manuscript. But the pull backwards was too hard to resist. Maybe there were clues to her own intimacy problems in Emily's past? Perhaps by understanding her own conflicts about intimacy she would be better equipped to help her readers sort out theirs? She did not know if there was validity to that theory, or if it was just an excuse for procrastinating on her new book. But she was compelled to explore her past further, and deeper, than she ever had before. Yes, she and her late therapist had tried to put the pieces of the puzzle together but, since his death, Emily had buried many of those old feelings and experiences. The title *Return to Intimacy* evoked so many thoughts and interpretations. Right now, for Emily, it meant the return to the childhood intimacies that had shaped her entire life as well as her relationship with food.

EMILY RE-READ HER DIARY from when she was ten, poring over the pages, searching for clues about what was happening to her at that time. Nothing was blatantly mentioned.

She did not look like a typical ten-year-old. She remembered being her full height by then—5 foot 6 inches. Since she had gotten her period already, she also showed some of the other signs of becoming a woman, like breasts. She looked a lot older than ten. So much so that her father got into a verbal fight with a cashier at a movie theater near their summer home. He refused to believe Emily was under twelve and sell her father a child's ticket for a movie, so they all left, in a huff. Her father must have been really mad because she also wrote in her diary for that day, July fifth: "Pop almost got a ticket," which must have been referring to a speeding ticket.

On August 25th of the following year, the Keanes stopped going to Emily's beloved blue-shingled summer home. She wrote in her diary: "We left the summer home. We are renting it to Mr. Clements for three years. We were all crying."

On her birthday, she wrote in her diary that she was afraid

she would not get presents from her brother or sister. "Even though I gave Martin a $3.98 hatchet & Dora a $3.95 fan mask I doubt if they'll give me a present. No one said 'Happy Birthday Emily' until I told them it was my birthday."

But on the next page, written in a stronger, tighter handwriting, she reported: "Guess what! Dora gave me a blue, bulk knit sweater. It cost $6.00. Martin got me a $3.98 Junior Miss kit. It has finger nail polish for the hands & lotion & clear nail polish, nail polish remover & pink nail polish."

On December 14th, a Friday, Emily wrote: "Mommy got a job as an administrative assistant. She is thrilled. I'm sick. Wed. night at 12:20 I threw up. I stayed home yesterday."

Going to the movies, studying for school and Hebrew school, reading books, writing in her diary, thinking about which boys liked her, playing with girlfriends, those were the activities that, on the surface, were consuming Emily during the year she lost her innocence. No one knew what deep secret she was coping with. No one noticed Emily was more introspective and depressed and less fun-loving than a pretty, bright, creative, and popular ten-year-old like her should have been.

Her brother was thirteen when the abuse began. He had lots of copies of magazines with pictures of sexy women stashed all around his bedroom—under the bed, under his pillow, in the closets. Martin was obsessed with his height as well as the bad case of acne he developed, especially after eating his favorite dish, spaghetti with clam sauce. Martin liked to talk on the phone and would do so for hours with his friends. He hung out with different groups of boys, including a neighbor who liked to shoot BB-guns in the backyard. Martin inadvertently killed a bird with a BB-gun and felt very guilty about that. He was also hanging out at the corner candy store with friends and smoking cigarettes, trying to be a "tough guy." At that point, he had a very short haircut, a crew cut. Despite his acne, he was handsome with distinctive features, big white teeth, and an intensity and romanticism that girls found very appealing.

Her older sister was going through a gawky stage at this point, wearing "chubby" clothes and hating it. Her mother also started her fixation on Dora's nose, trying to push her into having "a nose job" as many other Jewish girls with elongated noses were doing. Dora firmly resisted her mother's pressure to have surgery.

But Emily remembered, even at that age, she and her sister were going to a "diet doctor" because her mother was concerned about their weight. (Her cousin Rachel was also going to a diet doctor in her early teens because of her "weight problem.")

Dora was proud that their mother had gone back to work full-time. Having been home with three kids since the age of 24, Mrs. Keane had been very worried about "What's after thirty?" So, at thirty-seven, their mother finally began a career.

The sexual abuse, ironically, had started that first year her mother went back to full-time work in an office that was rarely nine to five. Most days her mother was gone seven to seven.

EMILY PUT HER BOOK research aside for a few hours to study what she'd learned about incest. The taboo against incest and against inappropriate touching or sexual conduct within a family (parent-child, or between siblings) seems to be a universal one extending to first cousins as well. Except for occasional historical examples, such as the marrying within the royal family in ancient Egypt, incest is banned. Some primitive cultures, so aware of the temptation that siblings pose for each other in adolescence, forbid boys from even walking near a female sibling or being left alone in her company. It has been proposed that the nineteenth century philosopher Nietzsche had an incestuous relationship with his sister Elisabeth, which may have contributed to his life-long loneliness, melancholia, and eventual madness.

In Emily's case, the abuse isolated her because no one knew about it and secrecy had its consequences. It further bonds those who share the secret while shutting out everyone else. If the secret involves abuse, the cycle is complete since the victim is most bonded to the abuser, and the secret, if revealed, would jeopardize that all-important intimate relationship, however inappropriate.

✦

EMILY WAS 17 WHEN HER brother announced he was getting married. She was a sophomore at an out-of-town college at the time. Emily was grief-stricken about his news. She felt betrayed. She hadn't even met his bride-to-be or been invited to the wedding. She was so distraught that she dropped out of college a few weeks before finals and flew out to California. She lost credit for that entire semester because of her rash act. Since no one knew about the sexual relationship she had been having with her brother, no one could help her realize that his marriage could have triggered such an explosive response. She was alone with her reaction and its consequences.

Help did not come soon enough for her brother. Emily believed, in her heart of hearts, that his judgment was impaired the night he was accosted by that gang. She now sensed that he was as traumatized by Emily's upcoming wedding as she had been by his marriage a few years before. Back then she failed to consider that her brother, the offender, also needed help, probably even more than she did.

EMILY KNEW HER WEIGHT loss accomplishment was now in serious trouble by bingeing and compulsive eating that was out of control. She sought support from those at the weight control center who had been helping her for the last two years.

"I can't stop eating," Emily confessed to Amanda during her next appointment.

Even saying the words felt awkward and uncomfortable. She didn't have the rapport with Amanda that she had had for almost a year with Olivia. But Olivia had left, gone on to a career in business. Emily had to find a way to work with Amanda. Although Amanda was not a trained therapist, she was supposed to know what she was talking about when it came to over-eating. She should be able to help Emily fight the demons that were once again rearing their ugly heads. Compulsive eating had dominated many of the years since she quit smoking fifteen years before. She had gone up and down the scale, mercilessly.

Emily could tell these were words Amanda did not want to hear. The expression on her face was strained and perplexed.

"Are you in therapy?" Amanda asked after tense moments of silence had passed.

Emily did a double-take. This was not the help she had hoped for.

"No," Emily replied, almost tripping over the word. "You may recall that my therapist died last summer."

"That's right."

There was an awkward pause.

"So are you seeing someone else?"

"No," Emily said. "I was hoping *you* could help me. I can't seem to stop eating. There's something about the trip to Europe that brought up deep-seated feelings about my childhood. But I'm aware of it, so I just need to find a way to stop the overeating."

There was a lengthy silence.

"Can you help me understand why suddenly I'm bingeing after doing so well for almost two years?" Emily asked.

"Come in more often," Amanda said. "That seems to help you."

"Sure, I can do that," Emily dutifully replied.

Emily wondered how having more appointments to weigh-in and discuss what she had or had not eaten in-between appointments was going to help her get at the roots of what was troubling her.

"Have you thought of hypnosis?" Amanda asked.

"I tried that once and it scared the shit out of me," said Emily. "Can't you help me through this?"

"I'll do my best," said Amanda. "I just thought that since hypnosis worked with some of our other clients…"

"Did you see that movie with Kevin Bacon?" Emily asked.

"Which one?"

Emily replied, "I think it was called *Stir of Echoes*. The one where his sister-in-law hypnotizes him and his mind starts playing tricks on him. It was an amazing movie and even though it eventually had a positive outcome, for the longest time he felt like he was losing his mind."

"It's not usually like that," Amanda reassured her.

"Probably not, but for me, hypnosis is not an option right now."

Emily left the weight center feeling discouraged and sad. The emptiness, the longing, the hunger was growing inside. She knew that her bingeing wasn't physical in the way that alcoholism seemed to actually attack the brain and the liver. Charles Jackson had described it in such detail in his 1944 novel *The Lost Weekend.* It was a compelling description of the impact of alcoholism on a man's life, mind, and body, and the basis of the classic movie starring Ray Milland. She could still see that scene from the black-and-white movie where Ray Milland, playing the part of the lead character, Don Birnam, hides a liquor bottle outside the apartment window, suspended down the side of the building by a string. She could see herself hiding candy around the house the same way.

Was her need to binge on food caused by an addiction to carbohydrates or sweets the way she had been addicted to nicotine, or as Don Birnam was addicted to alcohol? She needed to understand this process and this intense drive to eat non-stop, or she'd surely go mad, balloon back up to 200 pounds, or do both.

It wasn't as if Emily was sitting down and eating an entire chocolate cake or a pint of ice cream. Her bingeing was in spurts and it seemed to have different causes each time. It took so many forms but it revolved around carbohydrates and sweets. She'd start eating bread or cookies, and find she couldn't stop herself until she was full to the point of bursting.

Then it would only occur at certain times of the day, especially between two in the afternoon and six o'clock or until Greg came home from work.

In addition to the compulsive overeating, there were other ways that Emily's weight control program and goals were sabotaged. She had stopped measuring the portion of her protein for dinner so that she was probably having seven or eight ounces of steak when she was only supposed to have three or four at the dinner meal. She was also eating several additional carbohydrates each day even though she was only supposed to have one.

Little by little, she moved away from positive behavior that she knew helped her to stay healthy and fit, like drinking six to eight glasses of water a day, or exercising at least 20 minutes, even if all she did was dance in the house.

The next visit to the weight loss center, one of the new assistants, Beverly, overcharged Emily for an item.

When Emily returned home, she telephoned the center to point it out, and the center promised to make amends, next time. But during the next visit, they forgot to give her the credit, and Emily was embarrassed to make a big deal out of $7.50.

During that visit, Emily had to use her credit card because Greg told her to hold off spending anything from their checking account which was almost in the minus pool. She used the card to buy another six weeks on their specialized diet program, including the pill to control her hunger that she was taking three times a day. The bill for those additional weeks, plus the food she bought, special salad dressings, gourmet low-calorie tofu cheese-cakes and specially prepared chicken, turkey, and meatless patties, came to more than $600.

As she left the center that morning, thinking about that $600 charge on her credit card, something snapped inside.

"I'm trading one addiction for another," she said to herself. She had spent the last year working tirelessly to pay down a $14,000 credit card debt. Now she was using her credit card to pay for a diet program to cure her food addiction. It no longer made sense to her.

She decided she wasn't going to renew the weight program when she finished out these six weeks, hoping she could make a dent in taking off the twenty-five pounds she had already put back on.

But her compulsive eating was definitely getting worse. It was as if someone had attached a rope to a sled and Emily was tied down to it. She was being pulled along the icy paths; her will to fight was broken by the harsh elements and the difficulty of walking on the slippery trail when she could so easily be pulled along on the sled.

How much money had she spent losing the weight *this time*? Let's see. She started almost two years before and it was costing $500-$600 every six weeks. Although Emily had reached her goal weight after seven months, she stayed on the reducing diet instead of going on a maintenance program, which would have been free. Ever the perfectionist, Emily continued paying the fee as she kept trying to get down to the magical number of 132. That would have been exactly an 80-pound weight loss, rather than enjoying and maintaining the size 7 weight of 135.

The strict diet program she was on had cost her $4,000 the first year. And now she was spending at the same rate during the first half of her second year there, plus the cost of all the special foods that she was buying, spending $100, $150, sometimes $250 a week extra!

Meanwhile, the weight loss center that she had been going to didn't even try to find a way to help Emily when she asked for assistance. They did not answer her e-mails, or phone calls, or pleas for help that came between appointments. They just hadn't connected to her. The program worked when Emily was in her "diet mode" and somehow she was keeping all the triggers to her emotional eating in check. But the minute she reverted to misusing food for emotional reasons, the diet, which Emily had become very dependent on to provide her with structure and emotional support, no longer worked. It simply wasn't enough, and she couldn't stick to it.

AFTER EMILY PURPOSELY missed an appointment at the Center, Amanda finally called three days later. Emily had missed the appointment just to see if anyone noticed.

"Is everything okay?" Amanda asked.

"No, everything is not okay," Emily replied.

"What's going on?"

Emily explained that she was disappointed in Amanda and her revolving door staff.

"Now that I'm having trouble with my eating, no one's there for me. I feel angry. I feel betrayed. I feel sad that I was misled. I thought that you and your staff were really going to help me overcome my eating problem."

Amanda listened and offered a few lame explanations that Emily found completely unsatisfactory, such as "I don't really check my e-mail all that often" or "I was on vacation when you called."

Emily was shaking when she said, "I decided I didn't want to have a large private practice because I didn't want to have the constant responsibility of having to respond to clients needing me at a moment's notice. But when a client has a need, it doesn't matter if you're on vacation. You should at least have someone else covering for you while you're away so your clients don't feel abandoned. If a client calls me, or sends me an e-mail, I make sure I respond to that client within twenty-four hours, even sooner—immediately or within an hour or two at the most—if possible."

"It sounds like you have some issues with me and I apologize for disappointing you," Amanda conceded. "I feel bad you're disappointed," she continued. "I'll give you two free months."

"That's a generous offer. Let me think about it and if I decide to take you up on it, I'll call back for an appointment."

Emily put down the phone, still shaking.

She ran upstairs to the bedroom where Greg was relaxing on their king-sized bed, watching TV. She told Greg that she was offered two free months. "What should I do?" she asked.

"Use your judgment," Greg answered.

That was one of the strongest ties she had to Greg, besides sharing so many of the same interests, sexual intimacy, and love for each other and for their children and cats. Greg allowed Emily to think for herself, to make her own decisions even if that meant making mistakes.

And he only once said, "I told you so," and that was when Emily took on a project that she thought she could do in just a month but Greg knew it would take many months, and lots of money, to finish it. He was right and she did spend thousands of dollars of their money to finish the research on that project and he did, that one time, say, "I told you so." But he didn't keep throwing it in her face as her parents used to do when she was growing up, and as they continued to do during her adult years about almost every major decision she enthusiastically shared with them (like could they afford to buy the house they wanted in the community they chose to move to).

She told her mother about Amanda's offer.

"Take it," her mother advised. "Two free months? What have you got to lose?"

"Is that a pun, Mother?"

"Take the two free months even if you decide to quit after that," her mother added.

"It's not the money," Emily explained. "I've finally broken free of them. I no longer trust them and if I go back and two months isn't long enough, I could be back in their clutches for another two years. I'll be broke at this rate!"

"But you could also be thin again," her mother answered.

"Now that I feel they're only in it for the money, I doubt the program will work. It was working the best with Olivia, my first counselor, because I really had a rapport with her. I really felt she cared."

"So go back to seeing Olivia."

"Unfortunately she left to take a corporate job," Emily said, sadly. She remembered that Olivia had told her that she had to leave because she needed to make more money.

"No, somehow I have to do it on my own," Emily announced to her mother.

SO EMILY QUIT THE WEIGHT loss program she had been going to for almost two years. At that point she was up thirty pounds since *The Morning Show*—twenty since The Trip, and another ten since she returned. But it was "only" thirty pounds. She had gained and lost that in two months in her twenties. She could lose that again. And she could do it on her own.

She was sick of all the diets that had failed her. Her compulsive overeating and bingeing problem had presented itself shortly after she quit chain-smoking fifteen years ago. In those years, she had spent thousands of dollars on diets that only worked for short periods of time before the weight crept back on.

There was that liquid diet. She had lost weight pretty quickly, dropping 70 pounds in five months but, as soon as she stopped drinking that liquid and paying all that money to the physician she had to see on a weekly basis, the weight returned with a vengeance.

Then there was that popular program that offered weekly group meetings and peer support. She had lost almost 80 pounds with that program. The weight came off more slowly than with the liquid diet and took about eight months to lose the 80 pounds. But she gained it all back within a few months of leaving the program. She had even tried working there but had to quit after a confrontation with another leader.

She tried a new program that made you buy their food. She was only 150 pounds when she started that program, hoping to go down to 135. But after one month of the intense regimen of *only* eating their foods, she rebelled and ate everything in sight. She was up to 170 within another month rather than going back down to 135.

A FEW WEEKS HAD PASSED after she quit the diet program and Emily was not doing very well with her weight problem on her own. She was still overeating compulsively. She ate anything and everything, especially the carbohydrates that she had been forbidden to eat for almost two years, except for one serving a day. She quickly became a fat, sugar and carbohydrate addict, craving cookies, cakes, cheesecake (she had only been allowed one dairy a day as well), ice cream, hot dogs on a roll (she had previously trained herself not to use a roll but to eat it with just mustard), chocolate, hard candies, cinnamon rolls, and lollipops.

Just like those years when she was a three-and-a-half-pack-a-day chain smoker and she seemed to be smoking practically every waking moment, the only time Emily wasn't eating these days was when she was sleeping.

It wasn't that noticeable when she had regained twenty-five pounds. But, by the time she put on forty pounds, her appearance began to change dramatically. The first major transformation was in her face. Her distinct features were getting blurred as her cheeks now blended into her ears, and her mouth looked smaller and less alluring in proportion to the expanded skin.

Her fingers looked thicker and more stump-like, and her ankles were bulging with extra weight as if she were wearing weights around her legs to improve her physical regimen. But these were not weights that she could buy and put around her wrists or ankles to improve her stamina; this was her actual flesh and fat that was diminishing her stamina because there was so much more fat and body mass to go through instead of just bones and vital organs.

Walking up stairs was becoming harder and harder; she knew she was putting unnecessary extra strain on her heart and lungs and all her other vital organs.

Her upper arms became heavier, and her thighs thickened and widened, forming a sort of fortress protecting her vagina. She wondered if this was one of the reasons she gained weight, because when she was thin, and her thighs no longer concealed her vagina, she often felt vulnerable. Those feelings may have been compounded by the fact that when she weighed 135 pounds she wore shorter skirts and brighter, more feminine colors. Her attractiveness at this thinner weight was a double-edged sword. While she felt better about herself and her appearance, she also felt exposed and defenseless to anyone who showed an interest in penetrating her. The weight gave her a barrier and a line of defense against feeling helpless and susceptible.

She was now a size 12 and 165 pounds.

At that point, she stopped looking in the mirror.

Or getting on the scale.

She stopped watching everything she was eating, completely abandoning whatever self-control remained that she knew, deep down, was paramount to her weight control efforts. But she couldn't help herself anymore. Her eating was out of control.

Denial had given way to rationalization. "I'll start tomorrow," Emily told herself every day. Fortunately Greg didn't apply any pressure on her. He had his own weight challenges to deal with—he was fighting to keep off all the weight he had lost, 60 pounds, although only 10 had returned—and he also found Emily sexy and desirable, whatever her weight. They had excellent sex, despite Emily's weight gain.

There were no major TV appearances on the horizon that she had to worry about in terms of what to wear, what size dress or suit she was now, or whether or not her face would look bloated on camera. She had been invited to do an interview that would be put on the homepage of an Internet site, streaming video as if it was a taped TV interview. She respectfully declined, citing her busy schedule but knowing, in her heart, that she just didn't want to have her puffy face immortalized on the Internet right now.

Although this time her national television appearance and the trip to Europe had served as the catalyst to her latest binge, after each major weight loss over the last fifteen years, she could point to some trigger. First it was the way that the furnace man looked at her after she had finally lost the 75 pounds she had gained after quitting smoking and during her first pregnancy. That sexy look from the furnace man was enough to send her running to the refrigerator. She was all alone in the house when there were problems with the heating system and Greg couldn't get back from work in time to be there. One penetrating look was all it took to begin the steady climb that sabotaged eight months of dieting.

The next time was when she attended a training program soon after losing the 80 pounds she had regained. She looked stunning in the two-piece mini-skirted walking suit she had bought for the trip and, for the first time in years, she had felt the jealousy of other women about her appearance. There were two men at the training program, and one came on to Emily. It was her first time away from Greg and the boys for an entire weekend, and she found herself eating everything on her plate, as well as the candies that were put on each of the tables in the seminar room. By the time Sunday night came around, she was up at least five pounds and a binge had started which, just like this time, did not seem to stop, taking over as if it had to keep going until she regained all the weight she had lost.

The last time before this that she had lost the weight and rebounded was five years before, when she returned with Greg and the boys from California, all trim and fit, only to learn that her father had a brain tumor. As her father got thinner and thinner over the next few months, Emily soothed herself with food. By the time of his funeral five months later, she had to buy a new larger dark suit for the occasion, a size 14.

Her father gone, she was unable to feel safe at her childhood home with just her mother there. So without her father ready to step in and stand up for her when her mother criticized her, she decided to stay away during Shiva—the week following a burial in the Jewish tradition that family and friends gather to sit and share in the mourning process. Later, she wondered why she hadn't asked Greg to take the week off from work so he could be there for her through her ordeal and grief. But at the time, she did not think she had a right to ask that of him. After all, it was *her* father who had died, not his.

Cutting herself off from the comfort of friends and relatives during that Shiva week, she turned more and more to food to get her through that very hard time. There were so many unresolved issues with her father when he died. Her younger son, Stan, was only six at the time and Emily didn't have many options for babysitting. If she did get into Manhattan to visit her father at the hospital, it was just for an hour since she had to rush back to New Jersey to meet the school bus.

Emily felt guilty over the poor choices she made about how to spend her time during those months when her father was dying, just as she was making poor choices now about what foods to eat. She was eating things that were putting the pounds back on at the same time she was depriving herself of a chance to spend a lot of time with her father. With all his faults, Emily loved him deeply.

She had made peace with the fact that what happened with her brother was as much her father's fault as it was her mother's, the main object of her anger all those years. Her father had been emotionally distant, although he was probably closer to Emily than to anyone else other than his wife. But by letting Emily's mother get away with all the cruel things she did to her daughter, the plays she never went to, the recitals she missed because she "had a stomach ache," by not confronting her or requiring that she get therapy, he was an enabler to his wife's selfish behavior. He contributed to the family's dysfunction through his compliance.

Emily always knew that her mother was jealous of the relationship she had with her father. A gut-level competitiveness must have triggered words and deeds in her mother that, without therapeutic intervention to help her understand it, she could only act out. And yet, at the end, her mother paid tribute to that special bond between father and daughter when she called Emily at five o'clock that Friday morning, the same day that his son had died twenty-five years before.

"Daddy's gone," her mother said, tearfully.

It had been expected since his condition had dramatically deteriorated over the last week, but the finality was excruciating, nevertheless.

"Oh, no, Mom," Emily replied, crying. "Well at least he's not suffering anymore."

"I want you to go to the hospital and collect all his things. You need to sign the forms so they can release the body to the funeral home. Would you do that for me?"

"Of course." Greg and Emily told the boys that their grandfather had died but there was no reason for them to stay home from school that day. The funeral would be Sunday and it was probably better if they had somewhere to go and kept busy.

After putting the boys on the school bus, Greg, who took the day off from work, drove Emily into Manhattan to the hospital, to take care of the last details before the funeral director would take charge.

Her 80-year-old father was lying on the hospital bed, looking so small and frail; he weighed no more than 120 pounds and he seemed even smaller than his 5-foot 8-inch frame. His skin was already white and his eyes were closed. He looked like he was sleeping but there was no breath, no movement in his chest. Emily's legs felt like weights as she moved in slow motion in the midst of this surreal scene.

"We're all sorry about your father," the nurse said to Emily. "All the staff liked him."

There were tears in the nurse's eyes.

Yes, her father, who had but one friend besides her mother, was someone that people liked. He had been at the hospital for several weeks this time and until he became delirious a week before, he was able to have short conversations with the nurses and doctors.

Emily signed the papers and gathered together her father's possessions: his watch, an inexpensive one with extra large numbers that her mother had bought him so he could see the time more easily; the stuffed animal Emily had bought him when he was first hospitalized a few months before, when everyone was optimistic that they could shrink the brain tumor and extend his life by a few more months or even years; his gray striped bathrobe; and the photo collage Emily had made for him that he kept taped to his food tray that said "Best Grandpa in the World!" with pictures of Doug, Stan, and her sister Dora's daughter, Jean.

BUT THAT WAS FIVE YEARS ago. Over the past two years, Emily had finally lost the weight that she had regained during and after her father's illness. What was her excuse this time? A trip? Too much notoriety and success? That made no sense. Yet Emily had researched food addiction thoroughly enough to know that, ironically, it is when someone is most successful that he or she can feel the greatest amount of depression, self-doubt, and anxiety. Adult survivors of childhood sexual abuse often grow up with a complicated and negative attitude toward their bodies and toward food, misusing food to soothe the rage they feel inside for what was done to them. They also have mixed feelings about being attractive since they often blame their looks for their fate.

She understood all of that. So why was she still compulsively overeating? Although a few months before she was 135 pounds, a size 5, dancing as she walked, feeling light and feminine, she was now already up to 185 pounds, feeling fat, heavy, unattractive, and even scared by the health risks she was imposing on herself because of the extra pounds. Desperate, she went back to a popular program that had worked for her five years before. It was free for the first visit and she recognized a lot of familiar faces from her suburban community. It seemed more like a social club than a weight reduction program.

She stayed after the first half-hour lecture was over to hear about the program and what had changed since she was last there, five years before.

"Every food has been divided into a color category depending upon how many calories it has per ounce, with blue having the most, red the least, and yellow and purple in-between," the speaker explained.

"What about green?" Emily asked.

"So glad you asked," the speaker replied. "Anything that is colored green you can eat in unlimited quantities. Like water, most seasonings, condiments, et cetera."

"How do we compute the colors?" Emily asked.

"You all got your little booklet. Just fill in the rainbow for the day, taking the right proportion of foods from each of the colors, and, voila, without any effort, you will find that each week you'll be losing the weight slowly, steadily, and safely."

Emily bought books that gave even more detailed information and charts about what foods fit into each color scheme, for both generic basic foods as well as for eating out and for foods by brand name.

"Does it work, ladies?" the speaker asked in a voice reminiscent of a ringmaster at the circus.

"Yes," a quiet voice replied from the back of the room.

"Come on, ladies," the speaker admonished the group of 75

women. "Let's do better than that. Does it work?"

"Yes!" was the resounding reply.

Emily's head was spinning as she tried to figure out the complicated system, but she promised herself she would at least give it a try. That first week, she tried to create a winning food rainbow of blue, yellow, red, yellow, and purple that meant she was "following the curriculum" but it was proving very tedious. There were so many choices, she was still eating too much, and she was often confused over whether a particular food was "blue" or "red."

The next week, she returned to the ten o'clock meeting and got on the scale.

She had lost two pounds.

That depressed her. Emily remembered the times that she would lose five or ten pounds after the first week on a new diet. But then, again, she hadn't really been that strict that first week. She had "cheated" and it showed in the results.

The speaker explained that she had lost forty pounds by "following the curriculum," and had kept it off for four years, even though she used to binge and was a compulsive overeater.

"What made you stop overeating compulsively?" a blonde woman who looked like she had about fifty pounds to lose shouted out from the front row.

"I came here and started following the curriculum" the speaker replied.

Emily was disappointed by that reply. That was not the insightful answer she had hoped for.

Even though she had started the program the week before, she was still compulsively overeating.

The next week, Emily tried again to follow the program. But she just couldn't get into it. She didn't know if it was the complicated program or if she just wasn't ready to stop bingeing.

Back on the scale.

Up to 190!

"I've got to do *something*!" Emily exclaimed.

Her close friend Barbara had been bragging for years about the benefits of Alcoholics Anonymous so Emily decided to try again participating in Overeaters Anonymous. She had tried it years before and it just wasn't the right fit so she quit after a few meetings.

The meeting was in a church and after waiting alone for fifteen minutes, one man and four women arrived. It was a lunchtime meeting so they were invited to bring their lunch and eat it, if they wished.

Emily had brought a container of coffee but she knew she could not eat food in front of these strangers, at least not now.

Everyone who wanted to speak was allowed three minutes, and it was timed. Talking back and forth, or responding to what someone said, was not allowed.

Everyone shared the same problem, an abnormal fixation on food, but it manifested itself in different ways. One was a recovered anorexic, another a recovering bulimic, and the third was still overeating compulsively but grateful she had the program there to help her for the last four years.

The day that Emily went to the meeting, she had been "moderate"—*moderate* was defined as refraining from compulsive overeating—for several days. Emily announced with pride, "I've been moderate for two days."

Initially it felt very good to share. Emily spent $40 buying books about the program. She was enthused and hopeful. She held hands at the end of the meeting and together, with the other members, repeated the verse about how you will succeed if you believe in your success.

But instead of inspiring Emily to keep up with her moderation, somehow the meeting dragged her down. Going to a meeting every day to talk about her weight issues just felt too much like punishment. Her daytime hours were so precious to use for her work. Stopping to attend a meeting on a regular basis would mean giving up almost a day of "her" time to create and pursue her professional goals. She wanted to connect with new people, form new intimate ties, but she didn't want it to revolve around weight and compulsive overeating. Emily also didn't want a roomful of strangers to give her approval and friendship. She was sure this program worked for others, hundreds, maybe millions, but it wasn't going to work for her.

She found herself going back to compulsively overeating, feeling more alone and isolated after her brush with these strangers than she had before.

Emily wanted to learn how to feel genuinely comfortable with herself. She wanted to be able to enjoy her beauty and her accomplishments instead of being ashamed of her appearance. It was that shame that somehow seemed to reverse the success she had with dieting and achieving a figure and an appearance that other women envied, and men desired, to become obese and "big."

In Emily's mind, this was one of the most notable ways that her brother's sexual abuse had distorted her childhood and teen years. As soon as the abuse began, Emily began to feel ambivalent about her appearance. On the face of it, she was glad that she was pretty but on a deeper emotional level, she was angry and ashamed that she was attractive. Since the age of ten, Emily knew that it was her appearance, at least consciously, that was the reason her brother chose to sexually abuse her instead of her older sister Dora.

But was it only her looks that made Martin pick Emily, rather than her older sister, or was it because he knew Dora would not have gone along with him? There may have been something about her sister that told Martin that she would be the less likely victim.

Ask pretty women and they will tell you that they sometimes have to deal with the jealousy of less attractive women. That's a given. But to be ashamed and guilty about your attractiveness because of the havoc it has wrought in your life and your immediate family is the foundation for a much more powerful love-hate attitude toward something that should be a plus.

Emily recalled, from a very early age, wanting to please her brother, who was prone to sloppiness, so she spent hours cleaning up his room. She wanted so much to be liked and appreciated that she would do anything he asked. Over the years, she also put endless hours and much effort into creating scrapbooks for Martin as well as for her sister Dora.

Emily had felt ambivalent about more than just being pretty. She had mixed feelings about her brother's sexual actions—it felt good but she knew it was wrong. It gave her the attention that she craved, but it demanded her silence. This may have something to do with the ambivalence that sometimes plagued how she felt about friends, other loved ones and, from time to time, about even sexual intimacy. That was a theme echoed by other adult survivors of childhood sibling sexual abuse that Emily had sought out through support groups and for her research into the subject. At first, the sexual activities made them feel closer to the idolized older sibling or abuser. Only when they realized the dire emotional consequences did they allow themselves to realize that the sexual activities had been wrong.

She also thought of other inconsistencies in her life. She could work for hours on end and then have a writer's block. She could stay on a diet for months, never cheating, and then eat sweets for weeks. How might this be tied to the intermittent nature of her brother's molestation? It was especially unpredictable in the years before he went away to college at the age of sixteen, from ten to thirteen. At least after he went away, Emily could predict that the abuse would only occur when he was home on his vacations, usually three or four times a year, and only during the school year since he always spent the entire summer away.

It's also important to let anyone who has been abused, or who knows of someone who has been abused, know that the frequency of the abuse is only one factor in how that abuse impacted on someone's life and psyche. To be sexually abused even once by a respected authority figure is to destroy trust and create immediate and far-reaching dilemmas that have to be dealt with.

In Emily's case, the abuse was inconsistent, but persistent, over nine years. What the repeated abuse shows, however, is that there was a pattern at work. The terror and fear that even one incident of sexual abuse evoked was amplified with each incident.

Furthermore, as Emily learned the hard way, the sexual abuse became part of her expectations and experiences, similar to the battered woman syndrome. She often wondered if like some sexually abused children, she preferred the abuse to stopping it and then having to face whatever unknowns might occur. In practically all cases of abuse, the "cure" is to separate the abuser from the abused; if the latter is a beloved family member, the possibility of that occurring can be far more frightening than continuing to endure the abuse.

Looking back on those teen years, Emily was a good student and voted prettiest girl in ninth grade, but she was often sad. She had plenty of school chums but she did not have a best friend who would come over to her house or invite Emily over to her place. She remembered being very close with one girl who was also named Emily. They even shared the same birthday and were born in the same hospital. They were quite a pair. Emily was 5 foot 6 inches and a brunette and the other Emily was about 5 foot 2 inches and a blonde. But what was missing from their friendship, looking back on it now, was spending time together outside of school. They spoke on the phone every day but they did not do things together the way friends would if they enjoyed each other's company. Even though Emily lived only a mile away and she could even have walked there or visited by bicycle, their relationship was mostly on the phone after school and seeing each other at school each day.

In high school, when "the other Emily" went to another school, their friendship did not persist. Emily found a new close friend, Clara, but they also mainly spoke on the phone after school rather than get together to do things that most high school friends do together such as hanging out at each other's homes, visiting other friends, getting together at the local diner, going to the movies, or shopping.

Looking back, Emily wondered if they spoke on the phone because it was safer; face-to-face interactions had already become a power struggle for her.

Being a doctor, her father worked in a solo practice without other peers to relate to. That may have had a lot to do with the difficulty he often had relating to his children. It is one of life's great ironies that the traits that enable you to do your job well may be the ones that, unless you can turn them off, switch gears, and act quite differently, can be a detriment in your home life. Since some doctors dealt with the emotional aspects of their job by becoming numb to the pain of others, Emily's father also allowed himself to become numb to his children as well. Unfortunately, her brother's death only exacerbated her father's numbness, as he became bitter and angry in his older years in addition to being frozen and aloof.

When Emily was thirteen, she wrote a short story entitled "For Mother—With Love."

There were five hundred tenants in Sue's apartment building and the way they were monopolizing the party-line phone, she would never get that call through to her mother. That call, which would relieve tension and suspicion and put a new light on her vacation, would never be received. What was taking so long?

Finally, the phone was clear and Sue could dial the call that she had been waiting for hours in her hot and stuffy apartment. For once Mother was not on the phone gossiping and the line was clear. Her voice would soon be ringing in her daughter's ears.

"Mother, Mother is that you?"

"Yes dear," a shrill voice replied. "Is my little girl all right today?"

"Yes mother. I'm fine and so is Jim. How's Dad?" she grudgingly asked.

"Daddy's fine dear. I hesitate to ask you to come home but Mommy and Daddy miss you."

"Mother, I'm not a child. I'm thirty-five years old and married. Can't you realize Jim and I have our own lives to lead? We can't continue to live with you and Daddy!"

"Susie, we only want to let you know we need and want you. Now I'm going to cry."

Her mother began to sob, sobs heard all the way to Sue's room near Miami Beach, Florida.

"Please, Mother. Forgive me for being a naughty little girl."

"I know you're only going through a phase of growing up. You'll change."

"Yes, Mother. I'm sure I will change before I'm forty. I forgot to tell you Mother, the adoption didn't go through. We can't get Tommy, the little four-year old boy Jim and I both had our hearts set on. Why, Mother, why? We're the perfect family and we could all be so happy."

"Don't worry dear. You still have Daddy and me to take care of till we go. Don't you?"

The other end of the telephone wire remained silent. The silence of the dead. Susie lay there to be discovered by the morning maid. Her suicide would never be understood. What could have possibly driven her to disaster?

She had submitted that story to her ninth-grade English teacher as an obvious cry for help. But back then, teachers were not as aware of what to look for and respond to as they are today. Then, they often missed hidden indicators of possible problems at home in their students' writings and art works.

What Emily did not realize then, but she had become all too aware of in the years that followed, was that she continued to be suicidal. Instead of using sleeping pills, a knife, or a gun, she was killing herself slowly. First it was with her chain-smoking and, since quitting smoking, now with it was with food, overeating, and obesity. It certainly killed her self-esteem. And, when her weight got high enough, upwards of 180 or even 200 pounds, the likelihood increased that she could actually die from a weight-related cause, such as heart attack, diabetes, or high blood pressure.

OVER THE YEARS, EMILY and her mother had a strained relationship to say the least. On some days, they literally could not be in the same room together. When she was growing up, she and her mother were like oil and water. All Emily wanted was unconditional love and someone who enjoyed being around her, hanging out with her. But her mother followed in the footsteps of her own critical mother. Physical appearance, and looking beautiful, had always been a primary concern of her mother's.

Years later, when Emily was twenty-nine and on a book promotion tour, she wrote in her diary: "I went on television yesterday and I spoke to Mother, and she said, "Call me back if you look good. Don't call me back if you don't."

When Emily was growing up, her mother would scrutinize everything she wore, her weight, every pimple on her face, or every word she uttered. It was this incredibly mindboggling contrast of feeling like she was being spied on, but at the same time, feeling distant and unconnected, that were so hard to reconcile.

When she was thirteen something happened that probably helped to make it harder to break the silence and confess what was going on with her brother. It was also a good example of how children take a parent's thoughtless comment to heart, and how it can burn deeper into their soul than had been intended. She must have been walking around the house in a full-length white slip and nothing else. Her mother called her a "slut," and accused her of trying to turn on her father. She was ordered to dress more appropriately from then on.

Of course Emily should not have been walking around the house in a slip, but her mother's overreaction frightened her. If at that point she had any thoughts of telling her parents about what her brother was coercing her into doing, that incident stopped her. If she did tell her mother about her brother, Emily thought at the time, her mother would have confirmation that Emily was a slut. Emily's worst fear then was that her mother might have accused her of trying to turn on her brother, of "asking" her brother for their inappropriate touching, rather than being the victim of abuse. So she continued to keep the secret.

Looking back, Emily was now sure her mother did not mean what she said. Back then, when she got angry, her mother often had the habit of saying things like, "You kids will dance on my grave," or, "Your father comes first."

Now that Emily was a parent she saw how very hard it was to stop herself from blurting out "put-downs" or angry words when her children's behavior was exasperating or they were acting like "little toads," as her sister Dora used to call them. But it was worth the effort to control the impulse to blurt out such hurtful statements since Emily knew, first hand, even if a parent says, "I'm sorry," those put-downs lower a child's self-esteem and stay with them forever.

SHE'S WASN'T SURE WHO started calling her "Little Grandma," but the name stuck because Emily liked to do all the things her grandmother was good at, like sewing and cooking, things her mother often joked had skipped a generation. Dolores, who helped raise Emily, nicknamed her "Apple Dumpling."

Dolores, her Grandma, and her next-door neighbor Sally were her anchors during those early years. Her sister turned away from her at school, especially beginning in ninth grade when Emily, who had been a year behind, skipped a grade and was now perceived as invading her sister's turf.

Being in the ninth grade was challenging, but even tougher on Emily's self-esteem. She felt stupid getting a 94 on a test because there were geniuses who always got 100. But she still held her own. Emily and her sister even got together long enough to do an experiment for the science fair, winning Honorable Mention in the borough-wide event. They also pooled their talents, putting aside their sibling rivalry, by co-writing the school's first senior show. It was a parody and Emily was one of the co-stars. Writing and then selecting the students to play the other roles, as well as rehearsing and performing the show, was one of the highlights of her junior high school career. She could forget about the abuse and her brother as she worked hard and excelled in her schoolwork. She also kept her weight down by participating in sports: running, tennis, swimming, and gym.

When she was growing up, Emily always felt that her brother was the favored one, which made it that much harder to tell her sister or her parents what her brother was up to with her. She must have thought that they would have hated her for ruining their image of her brother. And what if he denied it? Looking back, to have attention from the favored one, even if it was inappropriate and damaging, must have seemed better than being ignored. There was also the element that she knew something about her brother that made him not as terrific as her parents thought. That secret gave her power. Reflecting on the past, Emily found that she just did not know definitively what she had been feeling at that time. It was hard to put herself into the mind-set of the frightened, angry, confused, and sad ten-year-old and depressed teenager that she had been.

Her mother bragged excessively about her brother. His every achievement, his every word, seemed to be such a big deal. Emily was jealous of that focus.

As she looked through the baby albums she saw many pictures of her brother, quite a few of her sister, and just a couple of her. She always felt she got whatever crumbs were left over after her brother and then her sister got their lot. She was sure a lot of youngest children felt that way, especially if there was only three-and-a-half years between the oldest and the youngest, and their parents had trouble relating to each child or being patient with them.

Emily thought about the time Martin brought his girlfriend from college to visit their family. She had flown in from her home in Minneapolis and she arrived at their house feeling very nauseous from the flight. But their mother was insulted that she had put out an elaborate spread of food and Martin's girlfriend was too sick to eat any of it. Emily did not remember Martin criticizing her mother for getting upset about the food, ignoring his girlfriend's ill condition, but he never again brought another girlfriend home. That was definitely a family pattern during Emily's childhood and teen years: instead of dealing with anger, the Keanes acted-out rage by pulling away, by disappearing, or through addictions like overeating or smoking.

Around that time, Emily lost her next-door neighbor Sally as someone she could rely upon. She had introduced Sally to another friend from school who lived around the corner. Unbeknownst to Emily, they started getting together without her. In time, they became better friends with each other to the point where Sally became unavailable to Emily. Once again, Emily did not speak up when someone important to her was doing something that upset her.

During her teen years, her mother was wrapped-up in her new business career and taking courses for her MBA. Her father was working harder than ever, as he would soon be facing three college tuitions almost simultaneously. Dolores was still working for the Keanes, although her hours were reduced; now she only worked three days a week instead of five, preparing most meals and doing all the cleaning and wash and ironing. Her sister Dora was busy with school activities and reading. Emily was also an avid reader and spent hours writing or doing craft projects as well. Her brother, Martin, was involved with organizing charity events, like a charity dance in Newark, as well as running for school office.

Martin seemed to live for his friends. When he was in elementary school, he was in car accident and was hospitalized briefly. The insurance company of the driver who caused the accident gave Martin $5,000 in a settlement for his injuries. It was supposed to have been made available to him when he went to college. But two years later, Martin wanted to buy a car with that money. His father objected, but their sister Dora, known as the family's problem solver, intervened and helped him get permission to buy the car. Emily and her brother always seemed to approach situations in a much more emotional way. Dora was the calmer, more rational one. She negotiated whatever dispute came to her attention between her parents and Martin, especially since he was going through a rebellious phase.

Her parents took her brother's rebellion during adolescence personally instead of realizing that most teens were going through it. They were angry with him for refusing to cut his long hair—which actually does not seem so long, by today's "pony tail" standards.

THE SCHOOL SHOW THAT Emily co-wrote with her sister received a standing ovation and she wished she had found enough positive attention from that, three years into her brother's abuse, to confide in someone and ask for help. It could have saved her six more years of fear and shame, and possibly even saved her brother's life. But she didn't. Maybe the writing was not yet a powerful enough alternative for her if, by telling on her brother, she risked losing his love and his attention.

Emily remembered so vividly going shopping for a prom dress with her Grandmother when she was fifteen. She was going to the prom with a senior, a basketball star, that she had been "going steady" with. It was a strapless light pink gown, cinched at the waist, with several red roses in the middle of the bodice with a stem going down the front of the dress. Emily wore a rhinestone tiara in her hair. She remembered putting a white sheet over the back seat of the car so her dress would not get dirty. Her brother drove Emily and her date to the dance and that did not bother her. She always managed to conceal what was going on between them when they were with others.

Her mother spent evenings going to business dinners and preparing for the next day. During Emily's formative years her mother was also preoccupied by attending classes for her MBA, as well as studying for those courses. Emily could not remember being read to as a little girl. Recently her sister told her that she was the one to look over her schoolwork and made sure it was okay, not her mother. Her mother was especially tense and unwilling to do family activities on Sunday, since she had to get ready for work on Monday and the rest of the week.

There were, of course, women who could have handled all of it: the job, the graduate studies, the three kids, the house, and the husband. But her mother was just not one of them. Someone had to be second fiddle in the Keane household and that duty fell to Emily and her sister. Dora seemed to handle it better than Emily did. Her brother was already in college just three years after her mother began her business career.

In high school Emily threw herself into extracurricular activities. She went out for cheerleading because it was a sought after achievement, although she never became part of the cheerleading clique. Emily was proud she made the squad and enjoyed its rigorous physical demands as well as the attention she received at the games.

She was in a club for teachers and did volunteer work reading for the blind. She was features editor of the high school newspaper and created an occasional newsletter called *Freebies and Cheapies* on a single-spaced, mimeographed, legal-size directory, front and back, about what you could do for free or with little money in New York City. That column got her in a lot of trouble with her high school principal when Emily recommended that students see a play called *The Underpants* in Manhattan. The principal, who thought she was recommending a lewd show, called her in.

"But it's a play about the suffragettes," Emily explained.

The principal refused to back down and, without her parents there to support her or to validate her claim he gave her a harsh warning and threatened to expel her if she wrote anything else like that again. He also forbade her from writing and distributing any more future events columns.

Emily's high school years were divided between seeking attention from her academic and extracurricular achievements—and boys. She ran for school secretary and was crushed when she lost. The slogan that the winner used during her campaign was, "Emily Keane has everything. Give me this one thing and I'll do it well."

Emily was optimistic enough to have a party planned the night of the elections, assuming it would be a victory party. She invited her rival who, fresh from her success, actually attended. Years later, Emily decided that putting herself in such an uncomfortable situation probably stemmed from being sexually abused all those years in that it made discomfort part of Emily's everyday thoughts and existence.

She realized now the sexual abuse also probably continued because her brother felt powerful with her, since she always said yes and obeyed him. He did not have the same 100% track record in the real world, where he often would get turned down and his heart broken by loving someone who didn't reciprocate. Emily remembered how devastated Martin was when he broke up with his girlfriend from Minneapolis, but she did not know why they broke up. When Emily later spoke with an old friend of Martin's, she told her that Martin was in love with someone else, who actually wasn't in love with him, but that he was turned off by how available his Minneapolis girlfriend had been. It appeared that Martin was caught up in an unrequited love scenario.

Still, what Emily remembered most about her brother was his adventurous spirit and his writing talent.

One of the things she most resented about the abuse was never knowing what her life could have been like without the omnipresent depression and fear that the sexual abuse, especially by a respected, revered authority figure, did to her.

While Emily couldn't bring herself to tell anyone about what her brother was doing, she did confide in her sister Dora when she lost her virginity to her high school boyfriend. Dora immediately panicked and shared the news with their parents, who also overreacted. They forbade her to ever see her boyfriend again and sent Emily to a psychiatrist that her father found in the phone book.

Unfortunately, the psychiatrist turned out to be completely ineffective and unscrupulous. Emily now wondered if the diplomas on his walls, or his degrees, were real or fake. Not only did he say to Emily, "Your problem is that you say too much. Do whatever you want. Just don't get caught." He even gave her brother the key to his office so Martin could have sex with his girlfriends when he was visiting from college.

The psychiatrist decided the best way to handle Emily's parents was to tell them that she was still a virgin.

"Don't worry," he reassured them. "She didn't really lose her virginity to her boyfriend."

They bought the explanation but she still was not allowed to see him again.

Her brother Martin had gone from Boston University to a master's program in writing at the University of Chicago. It was there that he met his future wife. Eager to begin supporting his new family, he dropped out of school and accepted a job as a reporter and columnist for a newspaper in Richmond, Virginia, covering the crime beat.

It was on a visit from Richmond, during the six-month

period Emily was living at home between colleges, that the last incident of sexual abuse occurred. Martin and his wife Melanie were in two of the three upstairs bedrooms. Emily's parents were in another bedroom. Emily was in the third room. It was around one o'clock in the morning. She was still awake. Anxiety plagued Emily in those days resulting in chronic insomnia. Martin came into her room and she knew what he wanted from that look on his face. She had not seen him very often since he went out to Chicago for his first year of graduate work, or after he and his wife and son moved to Richmond. She had visited them once in Richmond, spending the night, but nothing happened during that visit. This was the first time since he got married that they were alone together, or that Emily saw that look on his face.

"Sshhh," he said, staring at her with his dark brown, piercing eyes. "We have to be quiet so we don't wake them."

The lights were off in Emily's room and in the main level of the house. In the dark, however, she still could make out his features. Most of all, she could see his hand, reaching through her oversized nightshirt, grabbing her breasts. He unzipped his pants. Then he took her hand and with his hand on top of hers, together they moved her hand as his private part went up and down, faster and faster. As usual, Emily, who was now nineteen, squinted her eyes closed, distancing herself from what was transpiring but at the same time delighting in the little moaning sounds of pleasure that she was causing in her brother.

He left the room and his distinct strong body odors left with him.

But there was something very different about this sexual encounter. Somehow, her brother's marriage cast their sexual activities into a new light. Even if Emily had been willing to go along with it for all those years when they were both single and were just a lonely, searching brother and sister, clinging to each other for emotional nurturance, she now felt dirty and enraged that she had suddenly become "the other woman" in his marriage.

The next morning, when Emily saw her sister-in-law, she knew she would never, ever, let her brother touch her in that way again. She had a bond with her sister-in-law that her brother's sexuality had violated. She had a bond that somehow seemed even stronger than the bond forbidding sexual contact between a brother and a sister. The bond was that you do not have sexual contact with someone else's husband. It was hard to look her sister-in-law in the eyes that next morning. It would actually take Emily over two decades to be able to finally tell her the truth of the sexual intimacy she had shared with her brother during her childhood and adolescence, and why and when it stopped when she was nineteen.

Emily had started seeing a new therapist three times a week within a few months of returning home from college. This time, her parents found the therapist through a referral and not just out of the phone book.

Although Emily did not have an excellent rapport with her second therapist, at least he was not as completely off-the-wall as the first one. Emily felt enough trust to finally confide in him about what she and her brother had been doing since she was ten, especially what had just happened the night before. Although, until that point, most of their sessions were spent in silence, Emily now broke the silence to tell him how upset she was by the inappropriate sexual contact her brother, a married man, had initiated with his younger sister.

Her new therapist took a strong stand on the matter, calling her parents and her brother into his office to discuss what had happened and to have Emily repeat what she had told him in front of them.

"Is what your sister saying a fair assessment of the facts and situation?" the therapist asked Martin.

Emily's parents sat numb and frozen, waiting for their beloved son to accuse his sister of lying and spreading false, vicious rumors.

"Yes," Martin said, as he started to cry and wail. "It's all true and it's just like she described it."

"I have to ask you to stop," the therapist said.

"I just have one favor to ask," Martin pleaded.

"Yes?"

"Please don't tell my wife," Martin cried.

Everyone agreed to his demand.

That night at their parents' home was indeed the last time Martin and his sister were sexually intimate with each other.

Emily continued to live at home and commute to college for a while longer. But she and her mother were constantly fighting. The tension was unbearable when they were both in the house.

"Either she goes or I go!" Mrs. Keane blurted out to her husband one morning.

"But the therapist doesn't think Emily is well enough to live by herself or in a dorm," her husband sheepishly replied.

"I don't care! It's her or me. If she's not out of the house by tomorrow, you will be, along with her."

The next day, Emily was moved to an enormous studio apartment in Smithtown, Long Island near Tyler University, where she was a junior. But Emily was afraid of being alone and was plagued at night with insomnia.

After her brother confessed his abuse in her therapist's office and promised to never do it again, Emily shifted her focus to herself. She lost the weight she had gained while living at home with her mother. She rode her bike to classes from her apartment, getting her legs in shape and trimming down from daily exercise.

Meanwhile, not only did her brother fail to get any psychiatric help to deal with his guilt and conflicts over what he had done, but no one thought about what it must have meant to him to suddenly have his sister cut off as a sexual source. Whatever his neurotic reasons for needing his sister in that way, for years it had served him in some psychological and sexual capacity. Without being offered a replacement, or some understanding, Martin was forced to eliminate that source of gratification whether he was ready to or not. .

But Emily was too concerned with her own depression and getting through each day to think about Martin's conflicts. She was in her own apartment, nineteen, a junior in college, isolated, scared, and lonely. Her sister, who had spent her junior year abroad, was now back at her Ivy League environment, completely involved in her own life. Their brother, who found Richmond and his newspaper job unsatisfying, had moved to Staten Island, hoping that being in New York would help his writing career.

Out of loneliness, Emily called a young man she had met when she had been apartment hunting in Manhattan. He remembered her and invited her to go with him to a party that weekend. She accepted and it was there that she met Tom, her first husband.

The relationship with Tom was certainly not problem-free, but it was clear that Emily and Tom loved each other. She was twenty and he was twenty-two. They were both strong-willed and reluctant to compromise, and Tom was especially overly demanding and a perfectionist. Despite this, three months after they met, Emily moved in with Tom, giving up her Smithtown apartment. They shared a $160/month, fourth-floor railroad apartment on Manhattan's upper West Side.

At that point, Emily stopped seeing her second therapist since they had come to an impasse about Tom. Her therapist told her the relationship would never last; Emily wanted to find out for herself and felt her therapist had crossed the line between therapist and authoritarian parent.

"I want to experience intimacy, not discuss it," were Emily's parting words.

It was two weeks before Emily and Tom's wedding. A week before Martin's fateful encounter with the teenage gang that would end his life.

Martin called Emily and invited her to a movie screening at the Museum of Modern Art.

"Okay," Emily agreed. Despite his abuse, she missed her brother.

They met and over a cup of coffee he told her how he had lost the job at a local newspaper and how fearful he was about supporting his family with a baby on the way.

Martin was scared. His job as a reporter was his main source of income—he rarely got paid for his freelance writing.

Once again, Martin begged Emily, not to "tell" their parents that he had lost his job.

"Maybe I'll become a school teacher," Martin said.

"Why not?" she replied. "You'd be good at that, and you could do it until your writing career takes off."

"I'd have to go back to school," Martin responded.

"I'm sure Dad and Mom would help you out."

Her parents had given Martin a check for $10,000 so he wouldn't be jealous of Emily's upcoming wedding.

"Dad wants me to cut my hair for your wedding," Martin continued.

"It's fine with me if you have long hair."

"Tom's parents won't mind if the best man looks like a hippie?"

"Tom's fine with it and I'm fine with it."

"Okay, then it's settled."

A WEEK LATER, INSTEAD of enjoying the preparations for her imminent wedding, Emily, Tom, and the rest of their families were picking out dark-colored clothes to wear to Martin's funeral.

When her father went to the funeral parlor to select the casket and give the director instructions, he was very clear about one request.

"Don't you dare cut his hair," Dr. Keane had demanded, and Martin was laid to rest wearing the long hair that had meant so much to him, hair that had caused so much conflict between him and his father. It just didn't seem that important anymore.

A NEW E-MAIL from Emily's editor jarred her back to the present.

Emily, how are you and how are you coming along with finishing up The Return to Intimacy?

Lisa

Emily checked the date. The e-mail was dated that day. "Oh good," Emily thought. "I can still look responsive."

Dear Lisa:

So nice to hear from you. How are you? All is fine here. Working hard on the new book. It's coming along. I know the deadline is in sight. It's looking good for meeting it.

Regards,
Emily

The e-mail from her editor helped get Emily back into reality and away from her childhood reflections. Maybe now was not the time to tackle getting back on track about her eating. She had a new book to finish. It was a major book, too. She would have to get back to watching what she ate when she could handle both the book *and* her food concerns, or better yet, when she finished the book. Besides, just how much more weight could she possibly gain in only a few more weeks?

Part Four

Hitting Bottom

S HE STARED AT HER naked body in the mirror after Greg and the boys had left her alone in the house. "I've got to do something!" she said aloud. It had been weeks since she had seen herself naked. When Emily had lost all the weight, she actually enjoyed staring at herself in the mirror. Now, she dreaded seeing the layers of fat that hung off her midriff and stomach.

At noon she left to meet her old weight loss coach Olivia for coffee at a downtown coffee shop. It was over a year since Olivia had worked at the weight loss center. They had kept up their casual friendship through occasional e-mails but this was the first time they were seeing each other.

It took courage for Emily to keep that appointment. The last time she saw Olivia, she weighed 135 pounds and was the poster child of success for the weight loss program. They even paid Emily to display her "before and after" pictures at the front desk for three months.

Greg and others who had seen the weight come back on in ten pound increments month after month had gradually gotten used to Emily's larger size. But those who hadn't seen her in the intervening months were amazed at the dramatic difference in her appearance.

Her vain side wanted to cancel but she needed to see Olivia and talk with her. Olivia had been so supportive this last time Emily lost the weight. Hopefully she could say or do something now to help Emily get back on track.

They arrived at the coffee shop almost simultaneously.

"You look wonderful!" Emily blurted out, doing to Olivia exactly what she hated having done to her, emphasizing the physical.

As Emily poured a cup of coffee from the self-serve bar, and sat down at a round table for two, she tried to match up what she meant to say with what she had said to Olivia.

"What I meant to say is that you're radiating and glowing. You look so happy!"

"Thanks. I'm feeling great."

There was a brief pause.

"And *you* look great, too," Olivia responded, politely.

"Thanks for being kind," Emily replied. "But I have gained back some weight. I mean, quite a bit of weight."

"But you *still* look great," Olivia said.

"I've got to do something about it, though, Olivia. But I'm not going to that place anymore. They couldn't help me now that I seem unable to stop eating. But please don't say anything to Amanda or anyone there. I want to maintain a good rapport with them even though right now I'm angry at them and not talking to them."

"I don't talk to them at all. Don't worry about it."

"So what's your secret?" Emily asked.

"Well, I guess I'm just pleased with how everything is going for me. Bill and I are seeing a therapist together and he's also seeing one separately."

"So you're still together?"

"No, the divorce was final three months ago. But I don't want to give up on him yet. However, I do have my own place now. I'll give you the address and phone number but I'm never home so it's still better to e-mail me or call my cell phone if you want to reach me."

"How's the job?"

"Fine. I miss working one-on-one with people but the money's three times as much as I was making there."

Emily sipped her coffee. She was hungry and wanted to get a chocolate-chip muffin or a cinnamon roll but she was embarrassed to eat it in front of Olivia. She remembered how her mother found the chocolate bars she had hidden in her desk drawer during the six months she lived at home, in-between colleges.

"But this calm in you," Emily continued. "It's quite noticeable."

"The therapist I'm seeing is amazing. She's really helping me."

"Well, it shows."

Emily thought for a beat and then blurted out, "Do you think you would share her phone number with me so I could start seeing her, too?"

"Sure, I'll give you her name and number. Do you have something for me to write on?"

EMILY RACED HOME, EAGER to make that call. She got the therapist's voice mail.

"Hi, my name is Emily Taylor. Your patient Olivia Lawrence and I just had coffee together and I was really impressed with the changes in her since she and I last worked together. She was my weight counselor at the weight loss program in Maplewood. I'd like to set up an appointment with you to discuss my seeing you professionally. I initially lost 77 pounds and kept it off for more than a year but the weight has come back on with a vengeance since I've been eating, almost non-stop, for the last few months. I need help and hope you can help me. Here's my home phone number. Call anytime. If you get my voice mail, let me know when would be a good time to call you back."

Emily left her phone number and went back to work.

Two days went by. No word from Olivia's therapist.

Finally, the therapist called back.

"Hi, Emily. Sorry it took so long to get back to you but I wanted to figure out who would be good for you to work with. Unfortunately, I can't take on any new patients right now but I have a colleague that I discussed you with and she thinks she could help you. Her name is Arlene Hardy. Here's her number. She's expecting your call."

Although Emily was disappointed, she also felt grateful to have some immediate hope of help.

Three days later, Emily was sitting in Arlene Hardy's office. It was the living room of an old house that had been remodeled so that each of the upstairs bedrooms had been turned into small offices for other therapists, six of them, all women.

The first session went pleasantly enough with Emily doing

most of the talking, highlighting the key issues in her life that might be behind her compulsive eating and this latest weight gain.

"I wonder how many generations of women in my family are going to have to deal with being overweight or obese before it is no longer a family trait," Emily began. "My grandmothers were both overweight. My mother struggled with going up and down the scale twenty to thirty pounds her entire life. My sister has a weight problem. I have a weight problem. My late brother had a weight problem.

"My grandparents on both sides migrated from little towns near Kiev in Russia to Brooklyn in the early 1900s to escape the persecution of the Jews by the Cossacks. My father's side took up residence in the section known as Brownsville; my mother's side, in East New York, about six miles away.

"My paternal grandfather was not very religious, having personally witnessed, as a child, Russian soldiers beheading older male worshippers in his synagogue. When he was 75, Dad told me had never been bar mitzvahed. My sister and I had both been bas mitzvahed, even though, back then, it was unusual for girls to have a bas mitzvah. The reason he gave was that his father had distanced himself from organized religion after what he had lived through in Russia.

"Dad was six and his younger brother was one when their 26-year-old mother died. He grew up not knowing why his mother had died. His father would never discuss it. He figured she had a heart attack or one of the diseases common in those days. It was not until he was in his fifties that his great-aunt told him that his mother had died from complications after she tried to abort herself. She was using a potent over-the-counter drug. She was in such horrible pain that the doctor gave her morphine. The actual cause of death seemed to have been an overdose of morphine unwittingly administered by her doctor or by a family member. No one was sure of the exact details of what happened. It was at a time when some ascribed to the philosophy that if a little medicine helped, a lot would help even more.

"At the corner candy store, word soon got out that there was a widower with two young sons who needed a new wife. A neighbor told her grandfather that she had a distant cousin in Milwaukee who was single, thirty, and Jewish. A match, or *shidduch* was arranged and Mildred became Dad's stepmother. They had a classic marriage of convenience.

"Dad had always told me that he felt his stepmother treated him like a stepson but she treated his younger brother Lance as if he was her real son. He felt his stepmother knew he would always remember his real mother, and she resented that.

"Dad spent weekends with his real mother's parents, taking the trolley to a stop near their apartment all by himself as young as seven. On Friday nights, his grandfather would take him to the Turkish baths.

"My paternal grandfather had a factory in Brooklyn with 25 employees that manufactured the plaster ornamental work that decorated buildings. But then came the crash of 1929 and grandfather lost his savings as well as his business as the demand for ornamental work dwindled. The change in their economic situation had a lifelong impact on my father, who was always overly cautious with how he spent his money.

"There was another situation, other than his grandmother's death, the financial reversals, and feeling responsible for his younger brother that seems to have shaped my father's formative years. Dad was accepted at Yale but his grandfather could only scrounge up enough money to pay the tuition. In order for Dad to attend, he would have to reside with his great-uncle and his wife, who were both physicians in New Haven. But they said 'no.'

"Consequently, Dad went to a city university. He never again felt he could turn to a relative for help or that he would attain the dreams he had set for himself. Instead of pursuing the music career he had wanted throughout the years he'd attended Julliard Music School, he settled for the predictable and more secure life of a doctor, even if his heart was never really into his work.

"My maternal grandmother arrived in America when she was two. I always thought Grandma's birthday was Independence Day. But it seems that was the day she was given for her birthday when she immigrated to the United States since no one knew her actual birth date.

"Mom was one of three children and she felt she was her mother's favorite and 'the good one.' A portrait of Mom, painted when she was nineteen, hung over the fireplace for most of my childhood as a testimony to my mother's undeniable beauty. She had thick, wavy hair, aristocratic features, a trim, athletic figure, and a flare for acting and playing the piano.

"My Mom's brother, the first-born male, five years her senior, seems to have gotten away with even more and was more spoiled than my mother. Meanwhile, Mom's younger sister was labeled 'the brat' by her own mother.

"Mom adored and worshipped her father, a handsome, kind, and generous occupational therapist. She was devastated when he had a sudden heart attack and died at the age of 45, when she was just eighteen. Mom grew up feeling as if the two greatest loves in her life were her own father, and then her husband.

"There was a lot of competition and stress on achievement in both of my parents' childhoods, a lot of emphasis on 'marrying well' with material as well as academic success.

"Dad was twenty-seven and already a practicing doctor at the time they married. He spent the next four years as a captain in the Army. Mom was unwilling to follow him around the country when he was stationed at various bases, as most women in similar positions were doing. Mom was in college and determined to complete her degree. I respected the fact that Mom was committed to her education and her own identity and did not abandon it all to cling dependently to Dad.

"My parents were very much in love in those early years, and that love continued over five decades. When Dad was overseas in North Africa, she wrote to him long detailed letters each and every day. Other soldiers were jealous of his daily love letters. When I was a child I discovered some of those letters in the attic. I was overwhelmed by the love Mom expressed, as well as how painstakingly she shared the details of her everyday life. Mom told me that she vowed never to write a letter after the War and she kept to that decision. She explained that she had done enough writing over those four years for a lifetime. Years later, when we went to camp, it was Dad who wrote one letter to all of us with carbon copies. As the youngest, I got the bottom copy, the one that was hardest to read. Mom always added a P.S. at the bottom of each letter but she never wrote more than a few words, holding to her decision that she would not write letters after the War.

"Mom was twenty-four when Martin was born. Dora was born a year later and I was born two years after that. So, within a three-year period, Mom, who was all of twenty-seven, had three children with a man who had been in the army, and away, for much of the first four years of their marriage. She never got to put her college degree to use—not for another thirteen years.

"After the war, my parents first lived in a tiny room in the back of her father's medical office. They lived there with my brother until my sister Dora was born. They got little financial help from either set of parents but Dad's medical practice was starting to prosper. They were able to move to a more spacious apartment. I was born there and Mom had often told me how my brother, when only three, was forced to walk next to the carriage, like a little man, with his sisters being pushed in the carriage. My brother was forced to grow up so quickly because we came along so soon.

"I had asthma until I was five. Mom told me I was 'allergic to my own cold germs' and that was what caused my asthma. Whenever I had an asthma attack, it made my parents very fearful since I could sometimes turn blue from the coughing fits. A doctor reportedly made a serum out of my cold germs, injected me with it, and I never had asthma again, or at least that's what I was told."

"What do you remember?" asked Arlene. This was the first time Arlene had spoken since Emily had begun.

"I don't really remember how the asthma stopped, except that one day I no longer had it," said Emily.

"Interesting," said Arlene. "Continue."

"Even though they had a huge apartment and Mom spent thousands of dollars having a professional decorator customize it, eventually, they were fed up with trying to get an enormous carriage and another child into the elevator.

"When I was six months old, my parents pursued the American Dream and found a new colonial house on a tiny plot of land—40 x 100—in a development in Maplewood, New Jersey. It was near a main road and only a twenty-minute drive from my father's medical practice. They bought it for $16,500 with a $4,000 down payment and a 4% Veterans mortgage.

"Maplewood was just forty minutes from Manhattan, by car, twenty-five minutes on the train, and accessible by bus, although it would take $1^1/_2$ hours as it stopped at every little town along the way. The other homeowners on the block, except the dentist who had the corner house where his practice was also located, were tradesmen or small business owners—a plumber, a construction worker, a florist, a furrier, a manufacturer of women's casual wear. It was a mix of religious and ethnic groups with half Jewish and the other half Italian-Catholic, Armenian, and Protestant. I always felt proud that my neighborhood was such a diverse mix of ethnic and religious groups. It was a far cry from the older, more rural parts of Maplewood, with a minimum of half-acre zoning, which was about a mile away and had larger, more distinctive and expensive homes. We were the 'nouveau riche' who lived in the newer developments, which were affordable and, from the outside, often looked like blocks of exactly the same house.

"Growing up in the 1950s and early 1960s, I felt connected to my block, to my classmates at whatever public school I happened to be attending, or to my classmates at my synagogue where I attended Sunday school. But my family was never part of any community organizations and, except for reading the local newspaper, I could have been living anywhere.

"Our family looked like that old television program *Father Knows Best.* Beautiful, college-educated wife, successful doctor husband, and three healthy, attractive young children. Mom often told me we were called the 'cats and pajama' kids because we would run in and out of the rooms of the house in our pajamas, chasing each other.

"My first memory was a 'screen' memory. I could still see myself on the front lawn of my home. I was about two years old. Mom was standing behind the screen door. Dad was walking down the street, carrying an attaché case. He turned into our front walk and instead of stopping to say hello to me as I sat on the grass, he went past me to kiss Mom. He never returned to kiss me. Instead, he entered the house, closed the door, and left me on the lawn, all alone. I don't even know if that event happened or not. But it was symbolic of the way I felt throughout my childhood, being passed over for my mother.

"One of my favorite childhood memories was the family vacation we took—one of the rare ones—when I was three. We drove to a cabin on a lake near Cape May, New Jersey. I can still see myself, my sister Dora, and my brother Martin in the thick, bright orange life jackets we had to wear, jumping into the lake and climbing up the ladder only to do it over and over again. I also remember taking a shower in an outdoor stall near the lake, and screaming as my father removed leeches that had clung to my body from the lake.

"Even though Mom did not get a full-time job until I was ten, I could not remember her as a presence in my life during my formative years. I often wondered where Mom was during those early years. The only activity we did together was on an occasional Saturday to go food or clothing shopping, or a movie once in a while as a family.

"The only other time I remembered seeing Mom in our home was when she was lying on her bed, watching television, and she invited me to watch with her. It was very rare. She sometimes had a bag of chocolates and together we would watch TV and eat chocolates.

"In addition to always reading medical journals in his spare time or taking courses to advance his techniques and skills, my father worked very hard, including every Saturday until three o'clock. He worked four days during the week and his one day off, Thursday, he spent doing volunteer medical care at a hospital clinic. Weekday nights, I was usually already in bed by the time my father returned home from work, around 9:30. He and Mom would then eat dinner; we were supposed to be sleeping but sometimes me and my sister, who shared a room with me, were still up, reading or watching a late night movie.

"We never ate together on weekday nights, but we ate three meals together as a family over the weekend beginning with Friday night dinner. We ate supper late on Saturday afternoon, and brunch on Sunday, around one o'clock. I could still remember the menus. On most Fridays our housekeeper Dolores would serve breaded fried fish sticks, mashed potatoes, a green vegetable, tossed salad, and Russian dressing made with mayonnaise and ketchup. Saturdays they would usually have Southern fried chicken. Sundays, when Dolores wasn't around, we would have a traditional Jewish brunch of lox, bagels, and cream cheese, cold cuts from the delicatessen, or order takeout Chinese food.

"After the early Saturday night supper, my father would relax in his bedroom, watching TV and reading medical journals and he would invite me to join him. I relished being together. It was my private time with my father. Sometimes my mother was in the room, but often she wasn't. Myer siblings were either in other parts of the house or visiting their friends. Even if he didn't speak to me, watching *Sea Hunt* every week with my father was our time together. I did not realize it at that time what an inappropriate situation it was for a developing girl to be in. My father never asked me to leave the bedroom, nor did he offer to watch TV in the living room.

"Although there were no plastic covers on the living room furniture, we were not allowed to sit in there. That room was 'for company.' We didn't have a family room yet, and the dining room was only large enough for the table, so all social activities took place upstairs, in or separate bedrooms. Even after the family room was built, during my teenage years, I do not remember my parents watching TV in there, preferring to watch in their bedroom.

"Looking back, I don't remember any really comfortable furniture in our home. Not a big overstuffed recliner to sink into. Everyone relaxed on his or her bed.

"Sometimes we had family activities on a Sunday. We would

go roller skating, or on my mother's birthday we would drive to Manhattan and go to a restaurant or a movie. Visiting Grandma's was a big Sunday event. We usually met our cousins there and spent the afternoon together.

"I feared my mother throughout my entire childhood and this fear was profound and kept me silent. I especially feared the consequences of telling my mother something she didn't want to hear. Whether she meant to or not, my mother made me feel as if she would yell at me if I did anything she disapproved of, from the littlest accidental thing to the biggest one.

"I recall very clearly how when I was eight I was practicing ballet in the carpeted living room. I did a pirouette, and my foot hit a very nice candy dish that was on the coffee table. The lid of the candy dish broke. I was scared my mother would punish me. When she did find out what had happened, I was sent to my room, and I had to stand in the corner for what seemed a very long time but was probably fifteen minutes. The fact that it had happened accidentally was irrelevant.

"The worst type of discipline I received from my mother, however, was actually her infamous silent treatment. It was crueler and harder for me to be ignored by my mother for hours or even days at a time when she got really mad than it was to be threatened or even, on occasion, whipped with a belt.

"There was nothing that unusual about my childhood in those early years except for my father's depression. It was caused by his real mother's early death and his lack of connection with his stepmother or his father. It made it impossible for him to relate to his son although he did remain devoted to his wife. I don't know why my father seemed to do better relating to his daughters.

"When my brother was thirteen, and I was ten—the year the sexual abuse first started—there was a birthday party in the backyard for Martin. My father could not figure out what to buy Martin for his birthday. He had given him some money and told him to go to the corner where there was a candy store with a counter and soda fountain in the front and toys for sale in the back. He was to pick out something for himself.

"Martin cried. He told me that he wanted our father to know exactly what he wanted.

"During all those early years, my father did occasionally spend time alone with Martin. They went to the fights together, and once they went on a fishing trip."

"That's all very interesting," said Arlene. "But let's get back to you. What was your relationship with your sister like growing up?"

"My sister and I were both attractive, in our own way when we were young. Dora looked more like Sophia Loren. I had more of a cutesy Brittany Spears or Kate Jackson type of appearance. Neither one was of us was prettier than the other, just different-looking. However, our parents did something called 'splitting.' We were each given traits *exclusively*. My sister became *the* smart and good one, while I was *the* pretty one and the brat. Actually, we both were smart and pretty in our own way. My sister would get a 92 on a test, and I might get a 90, but Dora was still 'the smart one' even though I had skipped a grade and started college at sixteen. One reason I think I got my doctorate in psychology was that I didn't really 'feel smart' until I was being addressed as 'Dr. Keane.'

"Dora was more independent from an early age. I remember the phone call to our parents that Dora was in trouble because she and her fifth grade friend Sandra were found wandering along the train tracks in downtown Maplewood. Somehow Dora, even then, found a way to get attention and nurturance from friends. Dora had often told me how terrible it was to be labeled 'the good one.' The tendency to label is of course very bad for someone labeled as 'the bad one.' But she would argue about the incredible stress of giving someone the positive label. 'You can never be *that* good. There's always been that stress. I don't think you ever realized that.'

"My sister also reminded me of how girls at camp would try to befriend both of us as a way to 'get to' our handsome, sought-after brother. Martin always had charisma and charm. Martin was also strong, healthy, and athletic. He went to Cub Scouts with a neighborhood kid whose father, a schoolteacher, was the den leader for the troop. But our father, because he worked so late, wasn't at all involved in Cub Scouts.

"Martin died before I could directly express to him the anger I felt toward him for what he had done to me from the age of ten till nineteen. Over the years, my belief grew stronger that Martin's death was tied to my upcoming first marriage; I think it must have stirred up conflicting feelings in my brother. It was a difficult idea to accept since I had spent so many years exploring, researching, and debunking the notion of victim precipitation— that a victim could somehow precipitate, or cause, a crime.

"I still believe that victims are not to blame for the crimes that maim, rob, assault, or kill them. But that does not rule out that a crime victim's mental state at the time of the crime could, in some cases, impair the victim's judgment so that he or she behaved differently with a criminal, perhaps unconsciously contributing to his or her victimization.

"There's support for this theory in studies of suicide, where external events, such as breaking up with a spouse or loved one, losing money, or being accused of or convicted of a crime, were directly related to failed suicide attempts or actual suicides.

"Being unable to express my anger at Martin is the confused way that many survivors of homicide often feel. How can I dwell on what was wrong with someone, or how angry I am at him, when he died such a violent, horrible death? When what he did to me couldn't have been such a big a deal since I'm alive and he's not?

"But I know it's crucial to deal with those angry feelings," Emily continued. "I now know they are legitimate feelings, whatever the sad fate of the person to whom that anger was or is directed–in this case, my brother.

"My goal is to get at the root causes of my weight problem so when I lose the weight again, I have some confidence that this time, once and for all, I will keep it off."

Arlene Hardy nodded and said in a soft voice,

"We have to stop, now."

Emily had no idea how long she had been talking. It could have been half an hour, forty-five minutes, or even an hour or more. She did not look at her watch.

"I'd like to leave you one of my books so you can get a sense of who I am from my writing," Emily said with pride as she began to remove *Forgotten Intimacy* from a fabric tote.

"Why don't you bring your book back with you next time," Arlene said, stopping her in her tracks. "I'd rather you show me your books as you discuss them."

"All right," Emily said, feeling rejected but giving her new therapist the benefit of the doubt that there must be a therapeutic reason for this approach. As Emily thought back on her own training as a therapist, she could not instantly come up with a clinical reason for her new therapist's action and words, but she was going to try to get past her rage and figure it out.

Emily left the session and drove to the health food supermarket four blocks away. It was on her way back home and she needed a few things for the house: milk, fruit, and vegetables. Emily hadn't planned on starting a diet yet so she also stocked up on some pastries, sucking candies, and chocolates, trying to pick the healthy versions of the fattening items, as if that would make a difference.

BACK HOME, SHE RETURNED to work on her new book until she met the school bus and the second part of her day, giving the boys an afternoon snack and being there for them if they needed her. It was distinct from the third part of her day, when Greg came home from his job in Manhattan and she prepared dinner and interacted with him in her other role as Greg's mate and friend. Her next appointment with Arlene was a week away.

The days until then blended together—working on her book after the boys were off to school, seeing clients, then meeting the school bus, dental appointments, doctor checkups, shopping at the supermarket, evenings with Greg and the boys.

The highlight of her week was having coffee with her new friend Jeanne, an occupational therapist. They had first met when their older sons were in the same class in elementary school. Their sons never really became friends despite a few play-dates, but Emily and Jeanne found they had a lot in common. They were both very driven by their ambition, their work, and having time for few relationships besides their husbands and children.

Their coffee at the local bookstore was an intense time. Jeanne and Emily brimmed over with news about their lives and activities that each one wanted to share. Emily was intrigued by what Jeanne's life was like as an occupational therapist, and Jeanne wanted to know what it was like to write a bestseller and appear on television.

WHEN EMILY FINALLY WENT for her second appointment with Arlene Hardy, she reflected back to how she felt when she was having coffee with Jeanne and previously with Olivia.

Emily filled the session talking about the pressures on her in finishing up her new book, her uncontrolled eating, her embarrassment that she had regained almost all the weight she had lost and that she couldn't seem to stop overeating even though, every day, she vowed that today would be different.

"You've had a lot of therapy before," said Arlene. "Fourteen years with your late therapist. You even have a doctorate in counseling. So I think it would be useful for us if you set a goal for your therapy with me. How can I help you?"

Emily froze. Her jaw almost dropped and she became mute for several moments. Then she finally managed to reply, "But I thought I had made it clear, first in my phone message and then in our first and now our second session, that the key reason I'm here is to finally unravel the reasons why I am overeating and can't keep off the weight so I won't rebound when I do manage to lose the weight again. Yes, I have had a lot of therapy. But I obviously still need help."

"I'll be away next week but I'll see you in two weeks. You could always leave a message on my service if you need to speak to me before then."

Emily said, "Have a nice week off," as she walked down the steep staircase from the tiny second floor office, through the living room, into her car, and back to the health food supermarket to stock up on prepared lunches and dinners, ice cream, oatmeal raisin cookies, and chocolate peanut butter patties.

The next day, Emily continued rehashing both therapy sessions. Something was missing.

"Connecting," Emily said out loud. "Arlene Hardy and I aren't connecting.

"And she didn't hear me."

She had told Arlene no less than four times that figuring out why she was bingeing, how to control, and how to lose the weight and keep it off, once and for all, were her reasons for seeking out a new therapist.

Arlene Hardy's questions showed Emily that Arlene might be feeling intimidated by her; and, on an unconscious level, Arlene may have been telling Emily that she did not think she could handle her. Of course, this was all speculation on Emily's part but, sometimes it's just such intuition and hunches that can save you from becoming a victim—propel you into a marriage that will thrive and last, or save you from one that is doomed to disappointment and disaster. She only had her gut instinct to go on but time was too precious, money too sparse, and her sensibilities too fragile to take the time it would entail to confirm those hunches. She had to act on them and hope for the best.

Then she thought some more about Dr. Peters. From the moment she met him, she was impressed with his intuitive sense, his ability to sum up what she was saying, and his direct insight into her emotions, as if he had known her his whole life, known Emily on a level she had never even known herself.

It was there from the start.

She could not settle for less.

She picked up the phone and called Arlene Hardy's voice mail, knowing she would probably be away.

"This is Emily Taylor. I want to thank you for your help so far but I don't feel we have the necessary rapport that's crucial for my therapy with you to be successful. This is completely subjective and I'm sure you help lots of people but I don't think you can help me. Just send me a bill for the two sessions and I'll pay you for what you've given me thus far. Good luck to you."

There. She did it. Emily trusted her instincts about someone. There was no right or wrong. It was instinct. She just didn't feel Arlene Hardy had the instinct or depth to take Emily on the journey she was now prepared to take, once and for all, to get at the root of her weight problem. She didn't want the Band-Aid approaches of "yet another" diet program.

She didn't want to hand over her free will to a hypnotist or a behaviorist.

For now, she was going to keep doing what she was doing. Eating. Overeating. Sucking on lollipops. Whatever it took to get her through the day. At least she was functioning. That was the definition of mental health when she took psychopathology in graduate school. "Is he or she functioning?" the psychiatrist teaching the course asked. "Can he hold down a job? Have satisfying intimate relationships? Then he's mentally healthy. You can't promise people happiness."

Yes, Emily was functioning. She was even happy. But she was consumed with a need to overeat, an overpowering need to keep regaining the weight she had lost, going back to the enlarged self she had once been, even though she knew that being thinner was better for her self-esteem, health, career, and stamina. There was no way she was going to appear in a bathing suit at her current weight, not even if she was guaranteed she would only be seen by other overweight women sitting in a hot tub. No, becoming obese again was definitely cramping her style, becoming a factor in the choices she was making, a negative factor.

It was now April first, almost ten months after Emily's dramatic TV appearance. Whereas she had weighed 135 pounds when she appeared on TV, she was now tipping the scale at 200. What started as occasional slips and then two weeks of falling off the wagon during the trip to Europe had turned into months and months of overeating, self-recrimination, false starts with new diet programs, self-hate, regrets, rage, anger, sadness, more compulsive overeating, bingeing, and depression.

No longer fitting into her tight jeans, tailored clothes, or her own sexy size 5 underwear, Emily was back to wearing her husband Greg's size 42 underwear as well as stretch pants with an elastic waist. She noticed that since the weight was back on her, she was dressing in the same clothes almost every day, sometimes for days at a time, only washing her pants when they got really "ripe," as Greg would put it.

EMILY HAD TO GIVE A speech the following week before 300 women in Connecticut. They had sought her out to be the keynote speaker at their "A Celebration of Sisterhood Day" after seeing her on *The Morning Show* so many months before. It was the largest fee for a keynote address she had been able to get for herself so far. She had decided to negotiate directly with the organization that hired her because she wanted to be involved in every step of the process as a learning experience, from the letter agreement to the expectations for her speech to the sale of books at the end of the talk.

Now the speech was approaching and it wasn't even a consideration whether she could fit into the two outfits she had worn to appear on *The Morning Show*. She had gone up at least five sizes since then.

The day before her scheduled talk, there was torrential rain in New Jersey but Emily was out, driving around, in pursuit of an outfit that could fit her the next day.

She drove to a large-sized women's specialty clothing store about twenty minutes from her home. Instinctively she grabbed off the racks several size 16 and 18 outfits, a combination of dresses and pants suits.

The 16s fit. She bought two. It was not a pleasant shopping experience. It was hard for her Emily to enjoy shopping for size 16 outfits when the last time she shopped for a public appearance she wore a size 5.

"When I lose the weight again I'll donate the clothes to charity," Emily assured herself so she would not feel guilty about spending money for outfits she hoped she would not wear more than once.

✦

BACK AT HOME, SHE STEPPED on the scale. Two hundred. That's a lot of weight but she didn't *feel* that big. When she looked in the mirror, she definitely looked different than she did at 135 and a size 5, but she was still pretty. She made sure she never left the house without putting on lipstick, rouge, mascara, and concealer under her eyes.

But men no longer stopped in the street and looked at her since her weight was back up to 200. The compliments from women about her weight loss or even about what a nice outfit she was wearing had also ended.

Emily's legs had become very heavy and much of her weight gain was in her thighs. It felt as if she were moving bricks or boxes of books every time she walked up the stairs. The varicose veins in her left ankle were exaggerated and even throbbing once her weight got over 180. Her breasts were sagging and twice as large as before, and her waist was thick and concealed with a drawstring where she'd been showing it off with a belt just months before. This was a far cry from the bouncy, athletic self she had become when she achieved her 77-pound weight loss. Only Emily's bloated face remotely resembled the glamorous, prosperous woman that she appeared to be on *The Morning Show* just ten months before.

Ironically, as Emily researched the amazing, incredible downward spiral she had been on, she learned that for those who have been sexually abused as children, it is when things are going very well for them that they may feel more depressed with self-hatred and anxiety. With that self-hatred came the accompanying compulsive need to overeat—or, for those with different eating disorders, the wish to avoid food, or to purge their meals.

Sexually, she felt much less responsive to Greg than she had become when she was thinner. Her libido was definitely being channeled into food and eating and away from love, lust, and Greg. They were still making love at least several times a week but Emily felt less intense. It was her fault. It was her excess weight that made her self-conscious and numb, even though Greg was able to satisfy himself and took the time to make sure she was satisfied as well.

✦

A CAR ARRIVED TO TAKE HER to Connecticut. This was the first car service to pick her up since the car to *The Morning Show*, ten months before. She was pleased she had required that round trip car service to Connecticut as part of her fee. Emily knew her limitations as a long-distance driver. She also knew that it was important for her to be focused on what she was going to say, and getting ready for the keynote address, rather than trying to make her away across bridges and through highways to a town in Connecticut about an hour from the George Washington Bridge.

She looked in the mirror and was pleased that despite the weight gain, the outfit she bought looked professional and attractive. Yes, she looked like a thicker version of herself ten months before, but she still had a pretty face and an appealing smile.

Emily arrived early. She was pleased she had beaten traffic and didn't have to worry about being late, but the hostess of the breakfast seemed more annoyed than pleased to have the guest speaker standing around.

"Hello, I'm Dr. Emily Taylor, the keynote speaker today," Emily said, extending her hand. "What's your name?"

One after one, she met those involved in planning the breakfast as well as some of the attendees.

Wow, Emily said to herself. She was feeling good, despite her weight. She had been self-talking for days about the fact that the women who were attending the breakfast were there to hear what Emily had to say, not to judge her by her appearance.

"The only one who really cares that I've gained weight is me," Emily reassured herself at every opportunity. "Show an interest in the women you meet. Give them something that might change their lives. Lose yourself for an hour. Focus on giving to them."

But there was no denying that Emily was scared about giving this speech. It was her most significant speaking engagement in years and she didn't want to blow it. No wonder studies showed that fear of public speaking was, for some, greater than a fear of death.

Even though Emily was a professional speaker and she had given numerous well-received presentations, it was hard not to dwell on those rare times that she didn't quite connect with the audience either in tone or in content. Those times were few and far between, but it was easy to flash back to failure and not to success with the stakes so high.

She had agreed to do this and she wanted to do the best job possible, whatever her weight. Whatever the outcome of this day, she was determined to give it her very best effort—all anyone could ask of her.

And that is what she did. For the next few hours, Emily put everything she had into her presentation, into her opening, her anecdotes, her statistics, and her answers to the questions that had been collected from the registrants.

At the break, Emily asked the audience to use the time to do an exercise.

"The topic of my talk today has been *Forgotten Intimacy*, which, as most of you know, is also the title of my book. So I want you to use the next fifteen minutes, our break, to find someone in this room you do not know at all. A total stranger. Seek that person out and I want you both to talk to each other, and keep talking, until you find something about each other that you have in common. Make sure you exchange phone numbers or e-mail addresses so if you wish to contact each other again, you will be able to."

Silence. Absolute silence. The moments seemed to drag on.

All of a sudden, there was movement, activity, as chairs were pushed in and women maneuvered from one part of the enormous ballroom, decorated with yellow, red, and blue balloons, to the other.

In fifteen minutes, when Emily had to stop the break and the exercise, there was so much talking and conversing that it reminded Emily of a Broadway theatre right after intermission, before the bell sounded to signify that the second act was about to begin.

"Ladies, ladies. I'm so glad you're all so enthusiastic about this exercise but we have to begin again."

Emily then concluded her presentation: "So, dear ladies, if I ask you, 'Is intimacy forgotten today?' what would you answer me? You have just seen what it takes to begin a possible new relationship that might become close, become intimate, someday. For intimacy refers to friendship as well as romance. Intimacy refers to feeling connected to your children as well as to your spouse. The exercise you did during the break showed so much about how intimacy begins. First, I created the opportunity for you. Then, you and someone else interacted and kept talking till you found something in common. I also asked you to exchange phone numbers or e-mail addresses so if you wanted to contact each other again, you could.

"But there is something you and the person you met—someone who was a total stranger to you an hour ago, but who is now an acquaintance and, perhaps, for some of you, a future friend, maybe even a close or best friend, or if you introduce this person to someone you know and they marry, maybe even a future relative—something that you and the person you met have to have that no one else can give you, not me, not even you. It is a chemical reaction to each other, a gut feeling that, 'I like this person.' Because you can't force intimacy. You can nurture it and help it blossom but the wish to be intimate with someone has to be there and it has to be shared."

The audience hung on her every word as she continued, without wavering, for the next forty-five minutes. Emily had prepared for this day. She had structured her speech and considered what themes she wanted to convey. She wanted them to listen to her and to hear her, to transcend her appearance and get into her mind and benefit from her decades of research and pondering.

Resounding applause completed her presentation as she ended with an original poem that she had written for the occasion, a powerful poem about intimacy that had come from her heart in one big gush the day before.

After the presentation she went to the back of the room where the 100 copies of *Forgotten Intimacy* were stacked. Emily had little hope of selling more than a half-dozen books, but she had humored the organizer of the breakfast by making sure at least 100 books were available.

Then, as if her late father and brother were reaching down from heaven to tell Emily, through this one experience, that she mattered, that what she had to say mattered, and that there was nothing more than this day, this moment, that she had to be concerned about, a line began forming to shake Emily's hand and to buy her book. But the women weren't buying just one book. They were buying two or three books, for daughters, for daughters-in-law, for friends, for mothers-in-law, eight copies for a Reading Group. When the signing was over, 96 books were sold. Over the years she had sold thousands of books but this was different. Each of these sales was because the women had been so moved by her speech that they wanted to learn more and, by buying a copy of her book, to also take a piece of Emily home with them.

A petite woman whose face had wrinkles and lines that prematurely aged her came up to Emily. It was hard to guess her age because of the sad look in her eyes.

"You know that exercise you had us do at the break?" she said in almost a whisper.

"Yes," Emily replied.

"That was very meaningful to me."

"I'm so glad," Emily responded.

The woman asked to buy books for two of her friends that she wanted Emily to sign. "My husband died two years ago and my son died ten years ago. AIDS. Finding new friends is important for me. Well, during the break, the woman I met—she and I kept talking till we found something we both have in common."

She paused again.

"And we discovered that we both have gay sons."

Emily smiled. There was nothing she could think to say in response to this woman's comment but it was an affirmation of Emily's worth as a speaker, a facilitator, and a thinker. She had connected with this woman, this audience, and it reaffirmed her decision to help herself, on her own, or find another therapist because she hadn't connected with Arlene Hardy.

Connecting is a gift, Emily thought to herself. Connecting is something that comes from someplace inside someone's core, someone's heart. You can work on it if you have to, for instance if a mother and child need to "work at" their relationship. It's certainly worth the effort since that is a primary relationship that can never be replaced.

But with a spouse, a friend, a therapist, a teacher, there has to be enough there instinctively between the two people that, in the end, all the work will be mutually appreciated since those new non-blood bonds cannot be forced.

AS SHE WALKED TO THE car for her return trip, Emily felt as if she had definitely hit bottom with her weight. She was more than 200 pounds, bloated, and dangerously overweight.

But this time she came to the realization that it happened for a reason. She realized from being able to stand in front of that group of women that she needed to feel powerful and important from within based on the core of herself, not her appearance.

She needed to get up in front of a group of people who were staring at her, watching her, evaluating her, just as they had when she was ten and doing that provocative dance at her brother's Bar Mitzvah.

But this time, it was appropriate. This time, she was in control. This time, she had decided that here was a good opportunity for her, for her career. It was not her mother inappropriately asking her to dance in alluring leotard and tights in front of gawking relatives, friends, and acquaintances, especially boys and men.

This was an appropriate place for Emily to be appearing and she had triumphed.

It all came down to her ambivalent feelings about exposure. Through therapy with Dr. Peters and her own subsequent intro-spection, Emily had been able to understand that because her brother exposed himself to her it had been difficult for her to get the consistent broad exposure for her books, which is necessary for success as an author. But because of her abuse as a child, exposure had had a mixed meaning. Understanding that, and becoming more comfortable with exposure, had been a pivotal step in her emotional and professional growth. Today's speaking engagement before 300 women, women who all represented Emily's mother on some very basic level, was a turning point. She knew it. She just knew it. Now if she could only feel it.

Emily got into the car for the return trip to New Jersey feeling good about herself. The depression and despair that she had sunk into after her victorious appearances on *The Morning Show* was lifting. The need to compulsively overeat and binge was starting to subside. For the first time in the longest time, Emily didn't feel guilty about her success. She didn't feel the baffling need to undermine her latest achievement, a need that used to be so great that, without the insights she finally internalized, would take over her as reflected in the compulsive overeating and bingeing that kept reoccurring.

But now, armed with a renewed feeling of self-worth and self-love, she was still left with the challenge of getting off those 70 pounds she had regained yet again. Unlike giving up alcohol, drugs, or cigarettes, she had to eat. She just had to learn how to eat in moderation. Depriving herself never worked, in the long term, so there had to be another way. Trying to stick to a strict diet was not the answer. It would work for a while but then she would rebound back to her old, compulsive habits. A way that might work was to find and practice a diet that allowed her to partake of those foods she enjoyed but in *moderation*.

Unfortunately, the concept of moderation was absent from her life. She never did anything in moderation. No, she had to find another answer. It had to go deeper than that. More than moderation, she had to recognize the feelings of fullness and fulfillment. If she felt full, she wouldn't be driven to eat.

Now, if she could only find those feelings of fullness. That's not always so easy in someone who so often felt so empty.

Part Five

Facing the Demons

AS SHE DID WITH SO many of her clients, Emily realized it was time to face her demons and to begin peeling away the layers of defenses she had created to avoid them.

SHE WROTE IN HER JOURNAL, "Hello, Martin." She then conjured up his image and a conversation with him in her mind that seemed so real, it was as if they were chatting around the dining room table in their childhood home:

> *"Hello, Emily," Martin replied.*
> *"What's it like in heaven?" she asked.*
> *"It's fine. A little boring, though. But now Dad's here."*
> *"I know. What do you do all day?"*
> *"I'm still doing a lot of writing. Dad and I play tennis at least once a day. Grandma spends most of her day cooking. She's still making that* shav *that we used to love. And the date-nut bread."*
> *"It sounds very pleasant."*
> *"It is," Martin continued. "Certainly nothing to be afraid of."*
> *"Martin, I want you to know that I forgive you for what happened."*
> *"Do you really have to bring that up?" Martin asked.*
> *"Yes, yes, I do. For my sake, and for yours."*
> *"You don't have to worry about me anymore. Remember, I'm dead."*
> *"But there's so much that was unresolved between us when you died. So many things I wanted to tell you. I have so many regrets, Martin. I am so angry with myself that I kept silent and ruined both our lives."*
> *"Emily, my sweet sister Emily. Now, at the age of fifty, it's unfair to harshly judge decisions you made when you were just ten. You did what you had to do then to survive. I was wrong. I was the older one. You looked up to me. I took advantage of you, your*

youth, and your complete adoration of me. I'm the one who should be blamed."

"But I don't want you to blame yourself anymore, either, Martin. That's the point. I want us both to be free of our guilt. To erase that past, that thing that bound us for so many years and so distorted my youth."

"You can't magically erase the past," Martin explained.

"But I wish it hadn't happened! I wish I could go back and redo my childhood, rewrite my adolescence."

"Then you would no longer be who you are because that was your childhood. That was your adolescence, right or wrong. It was the unique life that shaped you and that defines who you are now."

"Martin. Oh, Martin. I miss you so, every day, in so many ways. I thought after all these years the pain would be much less, the regrets, the self-hating. But it's still there. Help me, please."

"Emily, remember the story of Dr. Jekyll and Mr. Hyde, one of Robert Louis Stevenson's greatest novels? The tragedy is that by trying to keep the evil and the good apart as if they were two separate people, evil triumphed, destroying those who loved both men as well as the good doctor. Yes, I did evil and you did evil. You have to find a way to accept that and to forgive yourself and to realize that the same wonderful person who did magnificent deeds, also did the deed that you wish you had never done. You cannot rewrite the past," Martin continued.

"So what can I do?"

"Every time you regain the weight, and hate yourself because you are fat, you are letting your past win. You are reliving the self-loathing and, by becoming obese, you are making external the evil you feel internally."

"Help me, Martin."

"You have the answers, Emily. The answer is in believing that you deserve to be happy. The answer is in turning to yourself for love, not to food. You have to let yourself feel the pain. Cry the tears. Hate me. Get angry with me. You didn't kill me and you can't kill me. Fate is bigger than all of us, you, me."

"It's so hard," Emily cried. "The forces pulling me back are so strong."

"So you've got to fight harder to maintain the gains you make when you finally achieve what you want, Emily. You can do it. You can get back what you've lost and hold on to it this time."

"I wish I had as much confidence in myself," Emily replied.

"Why don't you? Look at the job you're doing with your children. You're not repeating the past. They're having the healthy, normal, positive childhood and adolescence that you never had. What a gift you are giving to them!"

Emily was silent for a minute.

"Thank you, Martin. I think I'm ready now for this new journey."

"Embrace the journey," Martin replied as he faded from Emily's mind.

As Martin's image evaporated a new realization filled Emily's mind. "Today is a new day." She continued writing in her journal.

Day One

Day One did not begin like any other day during the last eleven months that I was out of control. Day One began with me determined to turn my life around by taking charge of what I put in my mouth.

Step One. Get on the scale. My reality testing is the number on the scale: 203. That is my reality. I am not 175 or even 180. The reality is I now weigh 203.

Step Two. I knew I needed guidance. I wasn't a nutritionist or a weight loss expert but I wanted to try to get the weight off on my own this time. I did not want to give my power over to another program with a gimmick that might trick me into thinking that it was the device and the program that was the reason I was succeeding and not through my own efforts. But I knew that working with someone, a doctor, a nutritionist, a dietician, a therapist, those were fine options for others and, maybe even once again, for me. I just wanted to give it a try on my own the way I used to in my twenties when I might, from time to time, find I had inched up a size or two and had to take off ten or fifteen pounds.

Emily stopped writing and turned on her computer to access the Internet. She typed into a search engine the material she was looking for: "United States Government food pyramid."

Voila, within seconds, she had a choice of several versions of the food pyramid that she could access.

She clicked on the most recent version and was instantaneously transported to the website for the government's booklet about the food pyramid. There, for free, and in the public domain, were the guidelines for a healthy daily diet. There were three versions depending upon someone's activity level—sedentary, medium activity level, or very active. To her amazement, there, in black-and-white, with little modification, were the exact same guidelines that she had been given from the weight loss center that had been charging her thousands of dollars. Of course the government food pyramid didn't come with the one-on-one interaction of individual coaching, or the group interaction of the popular weight loss program based on weekly lectures and discussions. It would be just Emily and the guidelines but at this point, she already knew so much about dieting, and she knew there were experts she could turn to if she needed additional advice. Right now, for her, Emily's answer was depending upon herself for the answers.

She reread the recommended guidelines for the 1,600-calorie version of the diet. Since she was very inactive now, she realized she would need to lower that range if she wanted to reduce. She also had all the other guidelines from other diets she had followed that had, at least initially, been successful that she could turn to. She also knew that any diet, if she stuck to it, would work, if she could just keep the weight off.

But alas, now she was back to having to get it off in the first place. More than the calories, however, she needed to be looking to the guidelines for what she should be doing, and what she should be eating, to reduce.

The food pyramid guide suggested reducing the fat and sugars, increasing physical activity, and eating the lowest number of servings from the five major food groups in the food pyramid.

Day One and it was almost 2 p.m. and she hadn't had anything to eat. Just coffee. She was writing instead. Writing about her feelings. Writing about her goals. Putting into words the thoughts that had crystallized about how and why *this time* was going to be different from all the other diets.

There wasn't even any hunger yet, but she knew it would occur, and she had to be ready for it. Fruit. Vegetables. Healthy protein choices.

Bingeing on cookies, candy, ice cream. Those were the high-calorie foods she ate in excess and had made her fat. Those were the foods that were the tools of her destruction because it was so easy to regain weight eating those foods—and getting fat again contributed to her self-hate and feelings of failure.

They were the forbidden foods. And eating forbidden foods had consequences, like having a forbidden relationship. It may initially taste good, and offset the loneliness and anxiety, and the hunger, but it leads to self-loathing, regrets, weight gain, and concealed sensuality.

At age 50, Emily was determined to get her nourishment from relationships, from her sensuality, and from her work—not from fattening foods.

She missed out on getting the affection or attention she needed from her mother as an infant, as a child, and then as a teen.

When was she going to stop punishing herself or her mother for that?

When was she going to stop looking in cupboards and candy boxes for that love? When were real kisses going to be even more satisfying than chocolate ones? When was she going to be able to enjoy every food, even chocolate, cake, or ice cream, in moderation and without guilt?

When was she going to do what she had to do to lose weight and keep it off so she could get the self-adulation she wanted, and yet feared?

By regaining the weight, she eliminated the chance to work on her conflicting feelings about being beautiful and envied.

Now she was so obese she had even put her health at risk. The overeating and bingeing were nothing but slow forms of suicide.

Emily Taylor didn't think of herself as suicidal. She wanted to embrace life and rejoice in it, living as long as possible.

Could she accept that she could not undo the past but that she could rewrite the present and the future?

Could she learn to deal with success and exposure so it didn't throw her and make her uncomfortable?

Could she stop punishing herself for not saying "no" those many years ago so that she could enjoy her many successes today, without ambivalence?

Could she finally somehow get over the guilt of what she did and of what her brother did to her? Her brother's tragic death had nothing to do with her and everything to do with being in the wrong place at the wrong time, and the rage and criminality of the youths who stabbed and killed him.

Somehow she knew that "just knowing" wasn't enough. That "just forgiving" wasn't enough. Somewhere along the way, overeating had turned from a bad habit to an insidious addiction.

The NEXT DAY, EMILY AGAIN turned to her journal and recorded her thoughts and feelings.

Day Two

I got on the scale. Down two pounds. Those were two real pounds. Not because of an artificial pill, liquid, group, or chant. It was through my own hard work, based on my knowledge of what a healthy diet should be. The information was readily available to anyone who wanted it from the government, in books, articles, and even handouts from healthcare and nutrition associations or from dieticians, nutritionists, internists, and gynecologists. If I had to, I would return to a more structured program. Following the information, however, is far different than just knowing what to do.

I "owned" that two-pound loss.

It hasn't been easy.

I had insomnia last night.

Overeating helped me sleep. The food acted like a sedative.

I needed less sleep when I was thinner and I could go to bed later. That would mean more time awake, more time to deal with my feelings of isolation and fear as well as joy and pride.

But I am acknowledging the feelings this time, and feeling the feelings.

Not running away through food and self-destructive overeating.

Day Two Breakfast: one cup of fruit.

No snacks.

Day Two Lunch: Tuna salad with tomato and clear broth vegetable soup with snap green beans. An oversized piece of honeydew melon.

Day Two Dinner: Broiled swordfish and broccoli.

11 p.m.

Emily closed her journal and got up.

She went to bed but could not sleep after tossing and turning for nearly an hour.

How cruel this self-improvement regimen was proving to be. When she most wanted to escape into sleep, to avoid the time or need for overeating, her body actually rejected sleep.

She had a cup of low-cal cocoa, hoping that would soothe her, but the chocolate in the cocoa probably only stimulated her more.

"Back to work," Emily said as she went down to her office on the lower level, determined to write or do something productive rather than compulsively overeat.

Three hours later, at 3:30 in the morning, she was exhausted and ready to sleep.

Why did time seem to move so slowly whenever Emily was paying attention to what she put in her mouth? The minutes seemed like hours and each day seemed like a week.

Was it only Day Two? Had she been watching what she was eating for just two days? Months to go to get back to her goal weight of 135.

"I can't think about that," Emily reminded herself. "One day at a time, yada, yada, yada," she repeated, trying to cheer herself on.

"You can do it," she said, staring in the mirror. She noticed that even after two days, her face was beginning to have more defined features.

EMILY WAS DETERMINED to be kind to Greg and the boys even though she was restricting what she was consuming. She was not on a crash diet but even eating in moderation compared to her bingeing put pressure on her emotions. She could sense her increased tenseness but she was determined not to start picking on Greg or shouting at the boys, which she was prone to do during the early days of a diet.

Greg worked so hard. He deserved Emily in a pleasant mood when he returned home from his long commute. But they had a completely open relationship so she did not want to pretend everything was fine if she was having a tough time on the second day of the diet.

She decided to send Greg an e-mail letting him know how she was feeling:

"Dear Greg. I'm on the second day of my diet, as you know. It's taking its toll. Please forgive me if I'm a bit more short-tempered tonight. You know I love you. Please don't take it personally! Love, Emily."

Then Emily promised herself that she would count to at least ten, even twenty if necessary, if either of her sons got on her nerves. She knew the diet would diminish her patience and she hated to scream at either son. There was too much screaming during her formative years. She did not want that to be what the boys remembered about their childhood.

Day Three
On the scale: 198.
Down five pounds since I began to take control of my eating and to put myself on a lifelong healthy food regimen, just three days before. Out of the 200s.

Just nine more pounds and I'm into the 180s, although I feel depressed at the thought of the 135 I long for, and how far away it seems.

I'm not going to focus on how far I have to go. I'm going to think in ten-pound increments. All I have to do, for now, is get into the 180s.

That thought helped reassure her.

She went back to work, writing, focusing. She had cleared her calendar of as many appointments as possible, knowing, that as when she'd quit smoking, or stopped putting too many charges on her credit card, that that first week of radically changing her behavior was always the hardest one.

She discovered that compulsive overeating and bingeing was almost like having a light switch that she turned on and off. For months she had had her "self-control" switch in the "off" mode. Once turned off, she was shocked at how easily she slid into a major relapse, undoing what she had worked so hard to achieve three years before.

But now the switch was back in the "on" mode, and she was the one determining why and how she would eat or exercise, based on the knowledge she had gained over the years from research and being part of healthy eating programs. Now, she only had herself to thank or blame if this time she failed.

There was no pill or magic potion, no group, and no other person outside of Emily responsible for her success this time. She had joined a health club but she knew that she did not even need that to inspire her to exercise. She could run up and down the stairs in her home, or run around the house outside as her older son Doug was doing lately since he had started his own self-improvement regimen.

She was so proud to see 15-year-old Doug taking an interest in what he was eating, and exercising more. There had been a close call a few weeks earlier in which Emily nearly put Doug on the same path of looking for answers outside himself as had happened to her when she was thirteen and had been shipped off to a diet doctor for the first time.

Doug went in for a mandatory health check up and the doctor commented that he wanted Doug to lose weight.

"Here's the name of a nutritionist," the doctor said, "and here's the number at the hospital and the tests I want Doug to get to rule out any medical problems."

Emily took the piece of paper and left, intending to call the nutritionist and to have Doug undergo the tests.

But the next day, when she went to call, she found herself unable to pick up the phone.

Something felt wrong about this whole thing.

True, Doug was about forty pounds overweight, but was the path this doctor wanted to start him on the answer? What would be the lifelong consequences?

Emily decided, for now, to do nothing.

But within a few days, Doug, on his own, started to make changes in his approach to food and exercise. The first step he took was giving up soft drinks. He had been drinking three soft drinks a day. He started drinking bottled water.

Then, instead of getting side orders of mashed potatoes and gravy with the meals he ate out, he would get mixed vegetables without any butter or sauce.

Cookies and potato chips were also no longer daily necessities. He started working out at the high school gym as well as the health club's exercise room.

The changes were subtle and gradual, but noticeable. Emily was so pleased that Doug was doing it on his own. He would "own" those changes for the rest of his life. He was reshaping his body in his own time and in his own way so it was comfortable for him.

Of course, there are teenagers who may need to get those tests or seek outside counsel about what to eat, especially if their parents lack the knowledge about nutrition and healthy eating that Emily and Doug had acquired. But for her son, it was important that he end a family problem with compulsive overeating, bingeing, dieting, and regaining weight that seemed to have characterized both Emily's and Greg's sides of the family for generations.

Now that she was not overeating, and even though it was only her third day without bingeing, the world was definitely clearer for Emily.

Emily thought of her cats, Hercules and Cleo. Some years back, two elderly women had found Cleo abandoned on the street in Westchester. They brought the three-week-old kitten to their local animal shelter; Emily, Greg and their sons adopted Cleo a few weeks later.

By contrast, Hercules spent his formative first six weeks as part of a litter, nurtured by his mother, only removed from his mother and siblings to join Emily's family at the appropriate time.

Hercules and Cleo got along with each other but Cleo always needed more food than Hercules, begging for food throughout the day even if she was not hungry. She was always more fearful and less affectionate than Hercules. Hercules always showed very little interest in food, unless he was starving, and he cuddled up on Emily's desk or in her lap a half-dozen times each day. Cleo was more aloof although, in time and with effort and love from Emily and the rest of the family, Cleo had become a little more attached and loving.

But, over the years, Cleo's earliest deprivation still haunted her; Cleo weighed almost twice as much as Hercules.

Was Emily going to be like Cleo, always insatiable for food and love, weighing twice what she needed to weigh? Or was she going to find a way to reverse her earliest years and traumas so she could feel full enough within herself, emotionally, in her deepest core, negating the need to pile on the food?

<u>Day Four</u>
Weight: 197.
Down another pound.
I decided to keep this diary to help me through this renewed commitment to lose the weight and keep it off. I didn't know where else but in a diary to share my feelings and experiences. Yes, Greg is wonderful about letting me talk about what I'd experienced as a child, and how it had impacted on my life and on my weight, but telling him my feelings doesn't enable me to process those feelings

the way that I can through writing.

I write down my thoughts and explorations about the immediate and long-term consequences of childhood and adolescent sexual abuse among siblings. I can't change my childhood or teenage years and what had happened to me, but maybe I can find a way to help others to get over their pasts. Maybe I can help others to prevent it by understanding why it happens in the first place. Maybe I could help those with a weight problem, especially compulsive overeating and bingeing, to try to look for the roots in their pasts. That could help them to uncover the complicated reasons that they need to use food to soothe the rage, to fill up the emptiness they feel emotionally that seems like physical hunger but is really emotional hunger.

I know that children and adolescents are five times more likely to be sexually abused by a sibling than a biological parent, the more publicized type of family sexual abuses, but so few even know that childhood and teenage sibling sexual abuse is so rampant.

When sociologist David Finkelhor studied sexual abuse during childhood and adolescence among several hundred college students, he found 15% of the girls and 10% of the boys surveyed reported being sexually abused by an older sibling. This, as compared to 8% who said the offender had been a parent or a parent figure. In a study by Diana Russell, just 2% of the women who had been sexually abused as children said their offenders were their biological fathers.

Sibling childhood and teenage sexual abuse excludes the sexual curiosity between siblings who are close in age that is mild and considered "non-abusive." Abusive sexual activity is more dramatic, including oral sexual contact, fondling, touching, sodomy, or intercourse, although fondling and touching are the most common types of sibling sexual abuse reported, with the preadolescent ages of ten to twelve the most likely time when victimization first occurs.

Fortunately, my childhood and teenage sexual abuse by my brother never went further than oral sex or fondling. I am sure its effects would have been even more disastrous if it had gone further. But unfortunately immediate and long-term consequences of child-

hood and teenage sexual abuse were there nevertheless. My weight fluctuations and the difficulty I had when I achieved my goal weight (because that meant being looked at and noticed in a more sexual way) was tied to the mixed emotions I had toward exposure. There was still a deep-seated self-recrimination that I carried within my heart about what happened that ate away at the very real joy I felt in my personal life, as well as in my professional accomplishments.

Emily closed her journal, realizing she had learned so much about being a survivor of sibling sexual abuse through research as well as through joining a support group for other survivors. Through interviews and participation in that support group, she discovered that going through similar experiences, whether the perpetrator had been a brother, father, or stepfather, dramatically affected the other group members as well. The first feeling they all shared was a feeling of betrayal by a trusted authority figure. The second feeling was shame. Problems with weight and body image as well as sexuality and sensuality were also common.

For Emily, the immediate effects were to become depressed, guilty, self-hating, and withdrawn from her peers. The long-term consequences had been anger, shame, overeating, and overspending.

Being sexually abused as a child and adolescent scared Emily and distorted her early years. But it did not destroy her. She did not let it. But it did rob her of the joyful childhood and adolescence she might have had. However, through the hard work she had done in therapy for fourteen years, as well as self-analysis, she had been able to have a fulfilling second marriage. She had two sons with whom she had learned to be affectionate despite her initial fears of intimacy; better relationships with her sister and her parents, especially with her mother after her father died; and a writing, counseling, and speaking career she was proud of.

It had also been a crucial part of her recovery to accept responsibility for what happened. Although her brother used emotional coercion to convince her that she should do whatever he asked sexually, and that she should keep it a secret, she chose to comply. Although she would have liked to distance herself from what happened, in terms of the actual events as well as their emotional repercussions, she was a participant, even if an unwilling or ambivalent one. Her brother's sexual abuse involved an exchange. If Emily was to take complete responsibility for her life and herself, she had to begin to answer for the role that *she* had played in those nine years of abuse. This was through her compliance, through her secrecy, and through her distrust of her parents, her sister, or of any other authority figure to whom she could have turned for help, but chose not to.

Emily needed to share her story of childhood sexual abuse by a beloved brother so others could see how it happened to such an "unlikely victim"—the bright, pretty, smart daughter of a doctor and business executive whose schoolmates thought she "had it all"—and how it persisted for nine torturous years, undetected and unsuspected.

She did keep a diary for the first five years of the abuse and although there was no direct mention in any of those hundreds of pages of what was really going on between she and her brother, there were subtle hints. She didn't let anyone read her diary. But did she leave it around so someone could "accidentally" find it and read it?

Looking back, there were other ways someone might have been able to tell that something was very wrong with Emily and with her brother. It was below the surface, but it was there. The short story she'd written, "For Mother—With Love" showed great imagination, and yet someone in great despair, and suicidal.

Her hero worship of her brother was excessive and could have tipped someone off that something more than just brother-sister camaraderie was going on. After the abuse started, her brother used to look at her, even when there were others around, with an intensity and lust more typical of a lover than a brother. But no one noticed.

Emily also knew that she had to watch out that she didn't become a distant parent, hiding in her work, consumed by book deadlines and related pressures. She knew she could spend an entire day with her children—they'd be watching TV, reading, or having a play-date—and she'd feed them, drive them to their various activities, and talk to them. But they still might not have the "quality" interacting that makes someone's day, even if just for ten or fifteen minutes.

She had to constantly check herself and say, "Was I there for my children?" She had learned from the research that sibling sexual relationships that go beyond play into exploitation usually only occur in a family atmosphere that lacks warmth and affirmation.

Besides trusting her own gut instincts, Emily also knew the best way to judge how she was doing as a mother was to observe her children but also ask them, from time to time, "How am I doing?"

"You scream too much," Stan answered when she asked that question most recently.

Emily, rejecting her first impulse to be defensive, replied, "Thanks for sharing that with me, Stan. I'll try harder not to scream. I was raised in a family where my parents always screamed and I hated it, too. I guess I was doing it because that's what I knew as a child. But you're right. Screaming is wrong. Let me know if I'm doing better with that, okay?"

An open dialogue. An atmosphere that fostered feedback and criticism and, most of all, honesty and no secrets. Those were some of her goals for her children, for her family.

Day Five

Still 197. Still in the 190s. I've lost an incredible six pounds in just five days. My body seems to be on a temporary plateau, adjusting to the dramatic changes in my habits. I won't get discouraged. After all, in just five days the results have been astounding. I am feeling better and even danced a fast dance for a few minutes in the family room with Doug. What did I do yesterday that might account for this plateau? I have to be honest with myself—I've had too much fruit and I didn't weigh, measure, and write down everything I ate. I need to do that. Writing down what I eat helps keep me in reality.

<u>Day Six</u>
I decided not to get on the scale again this morning. Just focus on the program I'm following. I'm making myself crazy watching each and every pound.

I called my pregnant cousin Monica. She's due any day now. I had been struggling to call her because it's still hard for me to acknowledge other pregnancies since my miscarriage five years ago. My cousin is about to deliver and she's filled with excitement about the birth of her second child.

"I'm so excited for you," Emily said, meaning it with all her heart.

"Ann is pregnant with twins," Monica announced, sharing news about their other cousin.

"Great," Emily responded, but this time it was harder for her to feel sincerely joyful. First of all, she was not that close with this other cousin, only meeting her later in life, not spending an entire childhood together as she had with Monica. But twins! That was just bringing up too many feelings of loss and regret.

"Gotta go. Tell Ann I'm thrilled for her next time you speak to her."

"Will do."

Emily found that whenever her actions were in direct contrast to her previous victim behavior, she felt good about herself. Whenever she became passive and compliant, not only did bad things often occur, but she also felt bad about herself for backsliding to her victim role.

Five years ago, at the age of forty-five, Emily decided she could finally handle having a third child. Although she had had an excellent outcome with her Manhattan OB/GYN for her first two pregnancies, she decided to find a local physician since the commute to and from Manhattan would be tough with two kids. She and Greg had lived in Manhattan until Doug was four and Stan was one so having a Manhattan OB/GYN had made sense back then. Emily met the new physician, a woman around forty, who didn't seem to be married or to have children of her own. But that was not so unusual for female physicians, who often started families later so they could establish their medical practices before taking time off or reducing their schedules.

"You know, you're the oldest patient I've ever treated," the physician shared.

Why didn't that comment make Emily bolt out of there, beaming herself back into the office of the Manhattan OB/GYN who specialized in older mothers? Why wasn't that statement a red flag? Was it her old, misplaced trust in authority figures to do the right thing for her? Or something more like fear, or laziness?

"Stop being so paranoid," Emily had reassured herself. "This is a competent OB/GYN recommended by a reliable source. Everything's fine. Relax."

The physician warned Emily that because of her age she probably had a very small chance of getting pregnant again because of the decreased fertility that came with age. She did not want to hold out too much hope for Emily.

But within just two months of that appointment, Emily took a home pregnancy test that indicated she was pregnant.

"Come in for a blood test to confirm the results."

Emily went to the doctor's office, took the test, and got a call from the doctor's nurse the next day.

"Yes, Mrs. Taylor, you are definitely pregnant."

"I'd like to make an appointment to see the doctor," Emily said.

"Sorry, but she's booked up for the next few weeks. How were your other pregnancies?"

"Fine," she answered.

"No complications?"

"No."

"Then there's no reason to see you for another five weeks."

"But I really don't feel comfortable unless I get a complete examination the way I did with the other pregnancies."

"You were just here two months ago. There's absolutely no reason to see you before five weeks from now."

"Okay," Emily reluctantly said.

The next few weeks passed very slowly. Emily shared the news about her pregnancy with everyone and anyone. Except for her closest friends and relatives, who showed tact and compassion, almost everyone else responded, "Wow, lucky you, *at your age.*"

By the four-and-a-half week point, Emily's anxiety level was making it hard for her to sleep or even breathe. She had not yet been seen by her physician. Every time she called and asked to be seen the response was, "Are you having any unusual symptoms? Then just be patient till your appointment."

Desperate, Emily called every woman in town she could think of, asking for another referral. Emily didn't think to ask her original OB/GYN, based in Manhattan, for a recommendation in New Jersey, figuring, rightly or wrongly, that he might not have any contacts out-of-town. She was also self-conscious about giving up her first OB/GYN partly because the trip to Manhattan had become too time-consuming. In the midst of everything, she had gotten a call from an old acquaintance who had shared with her a very negative view of her first OB/GYN which gave additional reinforcement to Emily's decision to find a doctor closer to home.

A co-worker of her husband came through with the name of her OB/GYN.

"Come right in," the second OB/GYN said over the phone.

Within an hour, Emily was in the office of the second gynecologist, being examined.

"What a relief it is to see someone, finally," Emily exclaimed.

At last, after weeks of worry and fretting, Emily was getting her first prenatal exam for this new pregnancy.

"I have bad news," her new physician began.

"Is the baby all right?"

"So far the fetus seems fine, normal. But I discovered that you have a progesterone deficiency. It's easily treated with medication and we'll start you on it immediately. But I have to warn you that it might be too late. Since it seems this progesterone deficiency has been there since the beginning of your pregnancy, since it was not treated till now, there just may not be enough progesterone in the fetus' environment to sustain your pregnancy to term. We'll just have to wait and see."

"Oh," was all that Emily managed to utter, tears in her eyes.

"You know, progesterone deficiencies are quite common in older pregnancies. I'm surprised you didn't do a thorough test when you first learned you were pregnant since it is so easily treatable with drugs."

Emily felt numb. She knew it wasn't going to help her relationship with this new physician to badmouth the first one. She was also fearful of any legal consequences if she criticized the first physician and accused her of malpractice in not scheduling a complete physical exam and prenatal visit for Emily immediately instead of telling her to wait five weeks.

"I was a lot younger for my first two pregnancies," Emily said, trying to defend herself, "and everything went fine so I had no way of knowing there were developments to watch out for in my mid-40s that were not a problem in my mid-30s. No one ever talks about this stuff."

"You're right," the physician said, trying to gloss over the gravity of the situation with some doctor-patient small talk. "We need more education about the risks of older pregnancies and challenges, beyond just the decreased fertility considerations."

"Tell me what to do?" Emily pleaded.

"Take the medication and let's just see what happens. I want to see you again in two weeks."

Two weeks later, Emily returned for her appointment. "Everything's fine," her physician said.

"That's a relief," Emily replied.

"I'll see you again in three weeks."

At the ten-week check up, Emily had to bring Stan along. He was in all-day kindergarten at that point, but he wasn't feeling well that day so Emily had kept him home from school. But he wasn't sick; he just had a stomachache.

They had crayons and paper in the waiting room.

"We'll keep an eye on him while you're inside," the receptionist reassured her.

Emily donned her white paper gown, took off her undergarments, and hopped up on the table for a sonogram.

First the physician felt her stomach.

"Feels fine for a ten-week fetus," she said in a cheerful tone.

Emily sighed. She was the third child. Having a third child was very important to her on a symbolic level because she wouldn't be alive if her mother had stopped at two, as well as on an emotional level because Emily still had a lot of love to give to more children. She wanted to have at least a third child and, if possible, even more children. She loved having children and now wished she hadn't started so late, but who knew children were such joys? She had grown up parented by a very young mother who couldn't wait for her children to get out of the house so she could start "living" once again.

The physician put a cold gel on Emily's belly.

"This will help me get a better picture."

The instrument felt funny pressing against Emily's abdomen but she tried to focus on the sonogram image that she was watching on the screen to her right.

"I don't see or hear a heartbeat," the physician said softly.

"What did you say?" Emily asked, incredulously.

"I don't see a heartbeat."

"Should you see a heartbeat at ten weeks?" Emily asked, hoping that developmentally that was premature anyway.

"Yes, we most certainly should be seeing, hearing, a heartbeat by ten weeks."

She continued probing Emily's abdomen with the long-handled instrument.

"The baby's dead."

With those words, Emily let out a wail that seemed to start at her toes, travel throughout every pore in her body, and come out her mouth—a wail so loud she thought it would shatter the glass windows.

"Oh, no," Emily screamed.

She could hear Stan starting to cry in the waiting room.

She had to stop herself from screaming for the sake of Stan.

Now she was crying quietly, softly, tears streaming down her face.

My baby's dead, she said to herself. She felt as if someone had hit her over the head with a metal skillet.

"Where's your husband?" the nurse said who seemed to appear out of nowhere and who was now holding Emily's hand.

"I think he's in the air or his plane has landed. I'm not sure."

"What do you mean?" the nurse asked.

"He was on his way to California, on a business trip, to Los Angeles."

"Do you have anyone else who could come and help you?"

"No, no one right here," Emily said, regretting she hadn't put the time into developing a best friend here in town who could have been there for her in this time of need. Her chin was quivering and her knee wouldn't stop shaking.

"We always said Greg would never travel if I was pregnant. We made sure he didn't travel with the first two pregnancies. I don't know why I said it was okay that he went away this time."

"That didn't cause your miscarriage," the physician replied. "It's the progesterone deficiency that I warned you about. When babies abort naturally in a miscarriage, it's because something is wrong with the fetus or with the environment it's in. In your case, it could have been both. You have to believe that this is for the best."

Emily was still shaking.

"And it wasn't your fault," the nurse added, reading Emily's mind.

Emily would never know if there was a cause and effect between not being seen right away, having a complete work-up with tests that could have evaluated her for any problem conditions, and getting treatment for the progesterone deficiency, right from the start, would have prevented her miscarriage. There were so many reasons for miscarriage and many women, unlike Emily, had one or two miscarriages before they even had their first child. She had been lucky enough to have two pregnancies that led to two healthy births; it was only her third pregnancy that miscarried.

Still, it would have made dealing with it a tad easier if Emily had felt that she had stood up to that first physician and gotten her first prenatal visit and medical work-up the very minute she learned she was pregnant rather four-and-a-half weeks later. By then it was probably already too late to save the baby.

"Why didn't you order me to go to another doctor, one who would see me right away?" Emily asked Greg a year after her miscarriage.

"I didn't even know you were upset she wouldn't see you. I didn't know any of that," he replied.

His words helped her to understand that, without even realizing it, she had suffered, once again, in silence. She had been the silent victim. She hadn't even told her sister, her friends, her parents, or anyone close to her, not even Greg or Dr. Peters, that she was upset that the first physician wouldn't make time for Emily in her schedule right away.

That was why Emily felt it was so vital that she—and that other survivors of abuse or traumatic childhood experiences—work through the toll those experiences take on their judgment so that they can make better decisions in their older years.

Day Six

I 'm going to lunch with Greg's relatives later today so I've packed carrots and celery to get me through any "munchies." This renewed commitment to being in control is too important to let socializing or nervousness sabotage me.

I need to lose the weight, and keep it off, for my tired, overburdened feet, for my health, my heart, and my self-esteem.

That night, Emily tossed and turned, the dieting causing her to have insomnia again just when she longed for sleep. She had another dream that night. A disturbing dream. She was being pursued by a man who wanted to spend the weekend with her. She kept turning him down, but he was so persistent. The dream woke her up.

Day Seven

On the scale. Weight: 195.

The good news about lunch yesterday: I didn't go off my program! I carefully took one hamburger, no roll, a sliced tomato, and an apple for dessert.

The bad news: when a friend of Greg's nephew who'd come along for the barbecue said something that I didn't like, I didn't mince words but replied, "Up yours." Not a very polite or feminine way to talk to a twenty-four-year old boy.

—Sorry, I'm dieting, I said immediately. My apologizing with that excuse seemed to be accepted as completely understandable.

Every day represents new choices and new chances. By making healthy choices, I am stopping the self-abuse.

<u>Day Ten</u>
Weight: 189½.

Finally! Below the 190s even if only by half a pound. I've been using my writing to help myself through these early days and it seems to be working. But I'm also allowing myself to feel the feelings. I can't count how many times I've cried in the last ten days. Definitely more than at any time I can remember, except for when my father died and when I had my miscarriage five years ago. My eyes are sore from crying but I'll keep writing, working on the new book as well as my food journal. I need a place to keep track of my consumption as well as record my thoughts and feelings. It doesn't matter if anyone else ever reads this journal. It's helping.

Insomnia again that night. The dieting and weight loss were bringing up deep-seated emotions. She had another dream. She got up and stumbled around in the dark. It was just three a.m. Emily found the pen and journal she kept by her bed and scribbled down the details of the dream while she could still remember it:

There was a pregnant woman terrorizing everyone. I worked for the police. I had to capture or kill the woman. The first gun didn't work. The second gun fell apart. The pregnant woman gave birth to a baby the size of a hand. The police and I wanted her to give herself up. I was so weak and full of blood. But she wouldn't. I shot her but I did not kill her. I shot her in the leg. The baby was fine as well.

But Emily still couldn't get back to sleep after the dream. She made herself a cup of low-cal hot cocoa. What did the dream mean? Who was the pregnant woman in the dream? Since the woman in the dream was terrorizing Emily, would Emily have been justified in killing her? At least Emily was shooting back, not allowing herself to be the victim.

<u>Day Eleven</u>
Just trying to get through each day following the program of 5 to 7 ounces of protein, 2 portions of dairy, 2 carbohydrates, 3-5 servings of vegetables, and 2-4 servings of fruit. Weighing. Measuring. Planning each meal. Trying to avoid boredom and repetition by not preparing the same thing too often.

I gave my youngest son cereal for breakfast. My older son wanted a shirt and pants ironed before he went to school. I had done the wash the night before, no longer resenting household responsibilities as I used to. It's just two years till Doug will graduate high school and go out into the world, on his own, probably out-of-town to college. At least he won't have the ambiguous childhood memories that haunted me. Sure, the dishes from two nights before are still on the dining room table. That's why they had supper in the kitchen last night. At least the kitchen table was clean.

When Emily was growing up, Dolores, the family's maid, kept the house spotless, and always made sure that Emily, her siblings, and her parents had clean clothes that were starched and ironed. But at what price to Emily and her family?

Emily knew there was no single "right" way to take care of a household or raise children. Having a steady babysitter two nights a week so she and Greg could go out when the children were younger, and occasionally calling in a cleaning service when the grunge and heavy work became too unbearable, were Emily's solutions. She even treated herself to using the outside "wash and fold" service whenever she had pressing deadlines, or the piled-up laundry had reached the level of ridiculousness. It was a luxury, but at least it was not an invasion of her family's privacy, as would be a household employee who was not really family but not "just a maid," either.

She wondered where Dolores was today. She was probably dead by now. When Dolores retired from working for the Keanes' after twenty-five years, Emily never heard from her or about her again. She did not have a phone where she lived and no one gave Emily her address so she could write to her. No one even knew how old Dolores was when she retired. Her mother thought Dolores lied about her age when she first came to work for them; that she was really in her 70s and not her 60s, which would have made her in her late 80s or even 90s by the time she left. Since Dolores' mother supposedly lived to be 120 years old, that possibility wouldn't have been too farfetched.

Day Fifteen
Two whole weeks and one day of keeping myself in control. I'm getting out of the house if I feel the urge to compulsively overeat or binge, and that's helping me through each day. I'm also pouring my energies into work, finishing up projects I had been procrastinating on for the longest time. This is also deflecting my increased nervousness since I'm no longer allowing myself to eat whenever and whatever I want.

Three-thirty a.m. Emily woke up because of another disturbing dream:

I was becoming a photographer. I was supposed to take pictures at 7:30 the next Thursday of Dan Simon, a writer I know. I asked a woman to let me use her apartment and to be there with me. "If you know what I mean. I think he has a crush on me and I want you there for protection," I explained. I was also supposed to photograph a pregnant woman the week before. In the dream, I lived with a 75-year-old man. I was telling Dan Simon how fascinating it was to live with someone who knew Hitler. "I will get credits for the photographs," I explained. "My name will be on them. They will be published for literary purposes."

Emily woke up wondering, "Is my father the 75-year-old man in the dream?"

She got on the scale. Weight: 188

Down 15 pounds in two weeks. Not bad. A long way to go but she was on her way. Having disturbing dreams was one of the side-effects of dieting that she just had to put up with. Going back to overeating so she could sleep more easily was not an acceptable solution.

Day Seventeen

I'm starting to feel the need to go to a formal program for help with my weight challenge, but I don't really want to. I want to do this on my own.

I've already tried the most popular program, with weekly weigh-ins, several times before. When I last attended, I had reached my goal. Would it be belittling to me to attend again now, when I'm so severely overweight?

But is that really the question I should be asking?

No.

I'm going to use them. I have to stop worrying about what others think of me. Will that program help me to reach my goal? *That's the only question I should be asking myself.*

Emily went online and found out when a meeting was scheduled that she could get to.

"I'll stop by, see how it feels, and decide if I want to stay or not."

Day Eighteen

Weigh-in at the program and no one made me feel self-conscious that I'd gained so much weight since I was last there so many years ago that I had lost track.

The friendly faces were actually a welcome sight from the agony of trying to do this weight loss alone.

"Hi," said a familiar voice from the weigh-in section of the room.

Emily remembered the woman's face, but not her name. "Welcome back."

Emily got on the scale. She gasped at the weight since it was a full five pounds more than her scale at home. But she weighed-in at home without clothes, without having several cups of coffee or water, and first thing in the morning.

189. At least she was still below 190.

"You've taken the biggest step, coming back," the friendly administrator assured her.

"Thanks," Emily replied.

She sat silently through the meeting. She wanted to chat with the women to her left and to her right, but she was somewhat fearful that someone might say something to throw her off. It had been hard enough to return.

"I'll be friendlier next time," Emily told herself.

Day Twenty

I microwaved a prepared low-calorie frozen meal for lunch. I can have another company's frozen meals even though I'm going back to the other program. Mix and match, flexibility. That's what I'm striving for. I added some canned string beans to the prepared lunch, helping to extend the meal even further but for almost the same calories.

Day Twenty-One

The magical three-week point. It takes three weeks to form a new habit, so the popular thinking goes. Yes, I definitely feel that these new, healthier habits are replacing the destructive, compulsive ones I had adopted all those months. But the scale won't budge. It seems stuck on 188.

How many women are aware of the possible cause and effect between sexual abuse and obesity? Something like one out of three women are overweight or obese. Statistically, there are supposed to be only one of four women who were sexually abused as a child or teen. So I guess there's more to obesity than just childhood sexual abuse.

What about emotional abuse? Or that even more subtle but

equally damaging emotional neglect?

Was food trying to fill that hole, too? Do we turn to food to find the unconditional love that was lacking in our childhood and teen years?

Was it time to have the same kind of conversation with her mother that she had with her brother?

Emily was scared by the possibility that her compulsive over-eating would return with a vengeance. Her "conversation" with Martin had inspired her to have the courage to avoid using food to fill herself up when the guilt and self-hatred returned. Unfortunately, the impact of that powerful dialogue was wearing off. The demons were rearing their ugly heads once again.

Years earlier, whenever Emily had suggested confronting her mother in person, her late therapist had cautioned her—no, he had *advised* her in no uncertain terms—against doing it. "You're not strong enough….yet," he would say. Well, Dr. Peters was dead and no longer there for her, to advise her or to stop her from having the courage to try her own self-healing. Emily typed in her mother's number on her new cell phone.

"Hello, Mom? I'd like to come over for dinner," she said.

"Why?" answered her mother suspiciously.

Emily breathed a deep sigh. "Does there have to be a reason? Other families get together just because they love each other and enjoy sharing their company. I just want to see you and spend some time together," Emily continued.

"Well, I'm busy right now," her mother said.

"Okay," Emily said, pausing before continuing, "When will you have the time?"

"I'm thinking."

There was a silence. It became an awkward silence pretty quickly.

"Yes?" asked Emily.

"I'm still thinking."

"How about this Friday night? Greg can watch the boys, take them to a movie. I can drive over to see you."

"Okay. But you're not expecting me to cook, are you?"

"No. Don't worry about it. I'll bring Chinese take-out."

"Sounds good."

EMILY STAYED BUSY THE next few days trying hard not to dwell on the upcoming dinner with her mother. She thought about all the times she had been alone with her mother since she went away to college and left home and she could barely count those on her right hand. Maybe never? Her father was always there and then, after she got married, she tried hard to make sure her husband was there as well. She did try to visit her parents without Greg once her first son was born, but it was a disaster. After about fifteen minutes, Emily's parents told her they were calling a cab for her. They wanted her to leave. No explanation. They just had had enough of their daughter and grandson.

She didn't try visiting again without Greg by her side.

Now she was not only planning to visit her mother without her husband, but her father wouldn't be there either. Even though her father did not protect her, she could talk to him more easily and, he was usually an intermediary between her and her mother who brought out very deep fear and self-loathing in her. She missed her father but dwelling on his passing was not going to help her to deal with her mother, who was still very much alive.

Emily stopped at the Chinese restaurant closest to her childhood home. It was the same restaurant that she and her family would visit once or twice a year, on a Sunday afternoon, for an occasional no-reason family dinner. The management had changed hands a couple of times; she did not know anyone who owned it or worked there but it still felt comfortably familiar after all these years.

AFTER FIFTEEN MINUTES, she gathered up her order of spare ribs, beef with broccoli, won ton soup, seafood delight, and chopsticks and drove over to her mother's house.

She had a set of keys but for some reason it felt more comfortable to ring the doorbell, like a visitor rather than the family member she actually was.

"Hi, Mom," Emily said, giving her mother a kiss on the cheek, hoping to feel a connection to her through this act of appropriate physical intimacy; but she felt nothing on her end, and detected no warmth emanating from her mother, either.

"You're here," her mother said as if she was surprised.

"Of course I'm here, Mother. I said I was coming over for dinner."

"Malcolm will be here in about an hour," her mother said, matter of factly.

"Malcolm? You invited Malcolm?"

Malcolm was her mother's latest boyfriend. They had been going out for about six months. It was more of a friendship than a romantic relationship, although Malcolm would have preferred a more physical and intimate connection.

"Well of course I invited Malcolm. I'm dating Malcolm. Why? Does it bother you?"

"No," Emily replied, automatically. Then, after a brief pause, she reconsidered and said, in a more adamant voice, "Yes, it does bother me. This was supposed to be a mother-daughter dinner. Just the two of us. A chance to talk."

"Sorry about that. You should have explained that to me."

Emily was going to do just that but she felt exasperated. She wanted to save her energy for the conversation she was hoping they might have over dinner.

"Never mind," Emily said instead. "Let's have the food before it gets cold. Malcolm can join us for coffee."

"If you insist," said her mother. "But let's leave some food for Malcolm, in case he's hungry and he hasn't had dinner."

"Fine. That's fine with me."

They sat at the table where Emily had been seated for so many years when she was growing up, but it wasn't the same with just the two of them, without her father, brother, or sister. Or, when she was a child, without Dolores, who was there most days, preparing and serving the meals.

"Mom," Emily said, her voice almost shaking, "I want to

bring some things up. They may be painful."

"So why bring them up?"

"Because I have to. I've been losing weight but I've hit a plateau and I'm afraid I'm going to start overeating again. I always thought I ate to fill up the emptiness I felt because of those nine years Martin molested me, starting when I was ten. But now I think it goes back before then."

"Did someone else molest you before Martin? Oh, no! Who was it?"

"No, Mother. No one molested me before Martin. But someone did abuse me."

"Someone sexually abused you?"

"No."

"Physically abused you?"

"Not really?"

"Then what, then?"

"This person abused me mentally and emotionally."

"What are you talking about?"

"This person abused me verbally and by withholding love. Or at least that's what I felt, but I was too young to understand it or talk about it. I just felt unwanted."

"Okay. I didn't know about this thing you're calling mental or verbal abuse but if you say it happened, and it was a big deal, I've got to know who did this to you."

"Come on, Mom. You're an intelligent woman. You have a master's degree. You have a college degree. You studied psychology. Can't you figure it out?"

"Do we really have to get into a guessing game?"

"Well, I'll at least tell you that this person was very important to me. In fact, the most important person to me when I was a baby, when I was a child."

"Are you talking about your grandmother?"

"No, Mother."

"Well who was it then?"

Emily put down her chopsticks and looked her mother straight in the eye.

"It was you."

"That's ridiculous," her mother sputtered.

"No it's not. You called me a brat."

"But you were a brat."

"You were always insulting me because I had a slight weight problem. But what was my weight problem? Maybe I weighed an extra ten pounds. You were always praising my sister as the bright one and I was the pretty one but the dumb one. You were always bragging about Martin and how perfect he was, but never about me. When I was thirteen, I was wearing a slip in the house, a slip that looked more like a nightgown, and you accused me of trying to turn on my own father."

Tears filled Emily's eyes. "What about what happened with Martin? What he did to me?"

"What about it?"

"Doesn't it bother you?"

"It bothers me that you think it was such a big deal."

"But it was a big deal."

"Okay. If you say so."

"But the bigger deal is that I put up with his sexual abuse, I allowed him to molest me. I allowed him to destroy my child-hood and teen years and to make me feel dirty and contemptible because I was too afraid to tell you. And, worst of all, you had no idea of what was going on. In your own home. Under your own roof. You were oblivious to it. For nine years. How could you have been so obtuse?"

"How could you have been such a tramp?"

Emily got up from her chair, strode over to where her mother was sitting, and pulled back her fist and hand, as if ready to punch her mother in the face. It took so much self-control and determination not to punch her mother that she ended up punch-ing the wall instead, bruising and bloodying her knuckles.

"I think you'd better leave now," said her mother.

"Not until I get some answers."

"Keep your voice down."

"Why?"

"Because the neighbors might hear."

"What are you talking about? We're in a house that is separated from the next door neighbor's by grass and pavement. We're not in an apartment house or even an attached house."

"But the neighbors might hear us."

"You're more worried about the neighbors hearing us having this important discussion than you are about helping your own daughter deal with this psychic pain that has ruined so many decades of my life and is at the bottom of my overeating."

"Come on, Emily," her mother said, getting that crazed, "I know it all" look in her eye that had scared Emily all of her life. "You are always looking to blame others for your weaknesses. You like to eat. You like to overeat. You have no self-control. You have no self-discipline. You're lazy. You don't exercise. It has nothing to do with me or how I supposedly 'mentally and verbally abused you' during your childhood, as you put it."

Her mother paused, took a sip of water, looked straight into Emily's eyes, and said, "Besides, you had a wonderful childhood."

Emily laughed. "I had an awful childhood."

"No, you didn't!" her mother exclaimed in a louder voice.

Emily took a deep breath. Her right hand throbbed from the pain of smashing it into the wall, and with all the calm and determination that she could muster, Emily turned toward her mother.

"Don't you realize? *I'm* the one who decides if my childhood was happy or not, not you. And I say it wasn't happy. Martin's dead, for God's sake. Doesn't that tell you anything?"

The slap came suddenly and with a power and momentum that Emily hadn't known since those early days. That was when her mother took a belt to her and her siblings as she hit them with that belt saying, "Wait till your father gets home," only to find that when their father returned, he did not hit them. He did not use that belt. He took whatever their mother said in stride and ignored the whole situation that had seemed so catastrophic to his wife when she had to spend just a brief time alone with her children between the time when Dolores left and her husband arrived back from work at night.

Emily instinctively put her hand over her cheek that was burning with pain. It felt hot to the touch.

Now the tears were rolling down from Emily's eyes. She didn't know if she was crying out of pain or out of the sadness that on a certain level, being slapped across the face by her mother was actually better than the numbness that she usually felt toward her. At least there was some kind of emotion going on between them, even if it was rage and anger.

Emily sobbed quietly, waiting for her mother to apologize. The silence only lasted a few minutes before Emily finally broke the silence with, "I think I'm going to leave now."

As she walked toward the front door, she was still hoping her mother would cry out, "I'm sorry," or she would rush toward her, hug her, and beg her forgiveness.

She closed the door, got into her car, and sobbed on top of the steering wheel. She was not sobbing out of rage or anger, but out of sadness. Sadness that she had taken so very long to finally confront her mother. Sadness that she had lacked the courage to stand up to her mother when she was ten, fifteen, or even thirty, and that so much of her life, she had feared this awful woman who, by chance, was her mother. Emily loved her mother even though she never felt comfortable when she was with her and she only felt loved by her mother on rare occasions, rather than all the time the way a child needs to feel a mother's love. But tonight Emily had chiseled away at some of her fear of her mother, and that was a milestone for her.

She suddenly felt anger at her late therapist for denying her this chance for so many years. She knew, in her gut, that she would have been much further along in her self-healing if she had had the courage to confront her mother as she had confronted her tonight.

Driving back home, a smile started to spread across her face as she thought of her loving husband and the two children waiting for her at home. No, Emily could not erase her painful childhood, or force her mother to be the affectionate parent she had always wanted, but at least she wasn't repeating that horror with her own children. At least they were having a happy childhood and growing up feeling the unconditional love that Emily now got from her husband, children, and closest friends, and even from her sister, but that she had never been able to get from her mother.

But she was not going to give up on her mother. Tonight was a start. As long as her mother was alive, Emily was going to keep trying to get along with her in a much more comfortable way and to see if there was a way that her mother could give her the praise and affection that she always needed and wanted.

But most important of all, Emily was going to try even harder to get from *people* the love she needed and wanted, and to give it to them, rather than turning to food to fill that emptiness. Or to let her overweight or obese self form a wall against the advances of men besides her husband that might make her feel conflicted or turned on so that she would have to confront her needs and make choices about how she would satisfy those needs, rather than have the choices made for her by keeping herself encased behind a wall of fat.

Emily drove for around fifteen minutes when suddenly she felt her back starting to ache. It was so excruciating that she had to pull off at the nearest exit, find a gas station, rush into the bathroom, and hold on to the sink with all her might. She took a deep breath and suddenly she realized what she had to do.

She got back into her car and turned it around, toward her mother's house.

Once there, she stood at the front door, took out her key, and let herself in.

"Mother?" Emily said as she entered the kitchen. Her mother wasn't there.

"You scared me," her mother answered, as she walked down the stairs from the bedroom level.

"What are you doing here?"

"I have some more things to say to you that I didn't get to say before," Emily replied, in a somewhat louder voice.

"I think you've said quite enough, young lady."

"No, I haven't."

Her mother glared at her.

Could you please sit down at the table? I need to talk to you."

Emily's mother sat down, somewhat sheepishly, and somewhat out of curiosity.

"Mother, I need to tell you things that I've been storing up for years, for decades. Most important of all, I want to know how you couldn't have known. My weight gain started when I was ten, around the time the abuse started. Didn't you ever wonder why I started to overeat uncontrollably?"

Her mother just stared.

"I had an excessively close relationship to Martin, too close a relationship. Didn't that ever make you wonder?"

No response.

"I wrote a short story in junior high school where the mother and daughter have such a negative relationship, characterized by secrecy, that at the end the daughter kills herself."

"I never saw that short story."

"I know. I can't blame you for that. I wonder why my teacher didn't ask if there was anything going on at home? I remember reading an article recently in *USA Today* about a teenager who wrote a story that dealt with abuse or something like that and they interviewed his family and found out he did have a family secret he was keeping from everyone. The story was his way of asking for help."

"But you never shared your secret. You never asked for help."

Emily sat down next to her mother. She took a deep breath and realized that her mother was right.

"No, mother, you're not shifting the blame to me. I was *only ten years old* when it started, for God's sake. I needed *you* to notice things that were going on, to be sensitive enough to something that was wrong with me, or at least to be the kind of loving, caring mother in whom I could confide anything."

"What do you want me to do about it now?" her mother asked.

The question stunned Emily temporarily. She hadn't anticipated getting anything from her mother, no compassion, no understanding, no regrets.

"I want you to say you're sorry," Emily said, finally.

"I'm sorry," her mother said, quickly.

"Say it like you mean it," Emily answered in a louder voice.

"I'm sorry," her mother replied, in a slightly more convincing way.

"I still don't feel like you mean it," Emily responded, sadly.

"And I doubt you will ever believe me, Emily, because I can't undo the past. I can't erase what you said—say—Martin did to you."

"Mother, you know he did it to me," Emily said, her voice even louder than before. "He confessed to it with you and Daddy there, in my psychiatrist's office, not long before he died."

"That's right. I think I'm remembering that now."

"So don't try to rewrite history with me the way you're almost always changing reality. It doesn't help me to get better if you do that."

"Emily, at this point in your life—how old are you now, 46, 47?"

"I'm 50."

"Okay, by the age of 50 you have to fix yourself. You've got to make peace with what I did, or what you say I did, and what Martin did."

"Mother, I want to have a positive relationship with you. Dad's gone so I can't work on things with him that I wish I had worked on before he died. But you're still around. I want us to...."

"Be friends?"

"No, I have friends. I want you to be the mother I always wanted you to be, loving, caring, non-judgmental. I want to visit you without feeling like I'm walking on egg shells whenever we're in the same room. I want to see you and not feel as if you are putting me on a scale in your mind, weighing me and judging me by whether my weight is within the normal range of my height or not. I want you to love me unconditionally the way Greg does and our two sons."

"That's asking a lot of me," Emily's mother replied, almost overwhelmed and bewildered by her daughter's request.

"Why is that?"

"Because I have loved you and taken care of you the same way I was taught by my mother."

"That's all you know, isn't it?"

"Yes."

"It's making sense now. The favoritism you showed the three of us, that's what your mother did. Your brother was number one and you were the brainy one and your younger sister was the brat. Just like me."

"That's right!"

"That's so very sad, Mother. Didn't you ever feel sorry for your sister?"

"No, because she *was* a brat."

Emily was suddenly exhausted and bewildered by her mother's stubbornness. Her mother just didn't get it—how wrong her grandmother had been in how she treated her three children. Emily's mother had accepted and acted on those behaviors that were passed on to her by mistreating her own children the same way. Suddenly Emily wondered if something had gone on between her mother and her uncle.

"About you and my uncle..."Emily started to ask but she quickly stopped herself.

"What did you say?"

"Oh, nothing," Emily answered, not yet ready to confront her mother with that question, aware that her mother was not ready to consider it. She wondered if her mother would tell her the truth anyway.

"I've got to go home now, Mother," Emily said.

"Malcolm should be here soon," her mother answered.

"That's okay. I want to get home."

Emily leaned over and gave her mother a hug. She hugged her as hard as she possibly could. Then she gave her a kiss on her cheek. Her mother tried to respond but her movements were awkward and forced. But Emily realized that her mother was giving her what she was capable of sharing. She just didn't have it in her to be loving and caring toward her children or passionate and sensual toward a man. She was still a beautiful woman and she still filled men with lust, but her mother was cold inside and didn't like to be touched.

Emily had stopped those patterns with her marriage and how she connected to her children. Now it was time to fix her misuse of the food she had used to provide her with the comfort and nourishment that she lacked for so long.

"I love you, Mother," Emily said as she left.

"I love you, too," her mother said. Then she added, "But I don't like you."

Emily stopped and turned around, and looked into her mother's eyes.

"But *I* like me."

Day Thirty

I decided to go to a program meeting but I didn't weigh in. Instead, I took them up on their offer that I could go to a meeting and opt out of a weigh-in that one time. I just wanted the camaraderie. I needed the camaraderie.

I was starting to lose my resolve to stay on my path and talking to the other women—it was mainly women although there was one man in the back of the room—made me feel less alone in this struggle.

Day Forty

Weight: 185

Finally. At least I'm going in the right direction. Time to call Mom to share the good news.

"I'm proud of you," her mother said.

"Thanks Mom," Emily said, as if she was suddenly once again a needy ten-year-old looking for her mother's approval rather than a successful 50-year-old best-selling psychologist, happily married with two great kids.

"I know this is hard for you but you're not giving up," her mother continued.

Who is this woman? Emily thought for a split second. This compassionate, caring woman was so different from the competitive, self-absorbed woman she had confronted two weeks earlier.

Time, and the loss of her husband, apparently had mellowed Mrs. Keane. When would Emily finally not only reconcile this new loving, attentive mother of today with the less-than-perfect, overwhelmed mother of her early years? Emily was working so hard on forgiving her late brother for all that had happened; was she finally also forgiving her mother? Had her confrontation somehow caused her mother to begin to feel closer to her daughter? Was losing the weight and keeping it off one way to show that she had forgiven her mother? By continuing to binge or go up and down the scale, Emily knew that her rage was still not dealt with satisfactorily. It was still being directed at herself. And she so wanted to feel emotionally lighter as well as be lighter.

"Thanks, Mom, for your support," Emily continued. She was working hard at staying in the present and realizing that forgiveness did not come so easily, but that she would try.

Day Fifty
Weight: 179

The talk with Mom obviously helped. I'm in the 170s. Now if only this weight loss program wasn't so boring. I need to find new low-calorie treats. I want to learn how to cook delicious low-calorie meals but it's unrealistic right now. Too many demands between family and work. I did start taking out Chinese food, but only steamed vegetables, chicken or shrimp, sauce on the side. I let Greg and the boys get the dishes they enjoyed. I just didn't eat them.

Day Sixty
Weight: 170.

Thanksgiving—but I managed to stay in control.

Holidays should be about people and connecting, with food in the service of that experience. It was still tough. I had to turn down my mother-in-law's pumpkin pie, which I love.

I did have a bit more turkey than I should have but when we got home I put on some music and danced around the house to work off those extra calories. It felt so good to be moving to the music, enjoying my body once again.

Day Ninety

Weight: 160

I got through the holidays without misusing food. I still celebrated without depriving myself. Moderation is key *became my mantra, whenever anyone asked if I was dieting.*

For the first time in my life, I'm not "dieting." I'm simply making healthier choices.

I'd been through this so many times I was prepared this time. I was careful to avoid the magical thinking that destroyed so many earlier attempts at weight loss and maintenance. I used to think that when I lose weight, my life will be perfect. "When I lose weight, I will be happier. When I lose weight, I'll never be shy when I enter a room full of strangers." Without the weight to protect me, I'm actually shyer.

Day 150

Weight: 145

I'm dressing so differently now, trading my black pants and dark t-shirts for light pastels—even a bright yellow, clinging tank top and short yellow suit. I bought it in a fashionable Madison Avenue dress shop one afternoon. I was excited to be back into a size 8.

I'm getting closer to my goal and have to remind myself that once I reach that goal, I have to hold it dear to my heart, like the precious, and fragile, achievement I know it to be. It's so easy to backslide. I can't let myself ever do that again. I know that it's too easy to go from "in control" to bingeing.

There was the missing link, the piece of the puzzle I had never grasped. I always told people, facetiously, that the reason I had to stop smoking completely was that I knew, if I ever had a cigarette again, I would immediately be back to $3^1/_2$ packs a day.

Why is it so hard to understand that being out of control with food is the same thing?

Of course, I need food to survive and could not eliminate it entirely, like cigarettes. But the greater challenge is to always gain control so I do not succumb to "giving in" or "losing control" over what I eat.

I know the consequences of losing control.

I know that one bagel with cream cheese and jelly is, for others, just a bagel with cream cheese and jelly. If I had the right mindset, it could be just that for me as well. But if I combine the food and the emotional tension and anxiety, it becomes the beginning of a binge that might last a day, a week or, like this last time, months and months, until I hit bottom.

Day 180
Weight: 135

Finally, Goal Day! Here I am, back to 135 pounds! I've been using all the help I could get. Yet it was still through my own hard work that I stuck to the weight loss program, my own healthy choices even though I also was using the weight loss program meetings and their dieting concepts as well as their reduced calorie products and the prepared frozen lunches of a rival company as aids. The weight came off faster this time—all 78 pounds.

This time I was so focused, so driven, it was less of a battle once I got past the initial week of going "cold turkey," withdrawing from the bingeing and compulsive overeating and especially from the cakes and sweets.

It would be hard for anyone who did not suffer from this problem to believe that I was capable of putting on ten or twenty pounds in just a week, but that was the reality. By the same token, once motivated and focused, I was able to take the weight off with determination and speed as well.

I believe I have internalized a better way to eat as well as how to deal with my anger, rage, regrets, and feelings. I've spent the last six months reflecting on the past, planning my meals and snacks, and exercising, as if it was the first time. Yes, it was a shame that I had to hit bottom in order to go back to where I was. But this time I began to really own my success, my physical changes, from the inside out.

Of course there is no guarantee that I'll keep the weight off this time, forever, but I have as good a chance as that happening now as I ever had before—no matter what program I had paid to follow.

The next day, Emily went to the beauty parlor for her touch-up and trim. Although she was supposed to do it every six weeks, she had let it go for four months this time. She was far less comfortable going to the beauty parlor since she had gained back the weight, and putting off her appointment was just a natural extension of how resistant she was to re-experiencing the humiliation she felt every time she went there, heavier than the time before. They had made such a fuss over her the last time she had lost the weight. They tried to hide it but Emily knew they all felt sorry for her when she'd regained it.

This time, when she sat in the chair, she looked in the mirror and recognized the beautiful woman staring back at her, the attractive, stunning woman that she could be and was intermittently before.

"Boy, you've certainly gotten the weight off again," Isabelle said as she combed Emily's wet hair.

"Thanks for noticing," Emily said, smiling.

She paused for a few moments, wondering if she should say something or not. She decided that swallowing her words had too often been the reason for her obesity so it was time to speak up.

"Remember when I put almost all the weight back on a few months ago and you said to me, 'You're still pretty on the inside?'"

"Did I say that?"

"Yes, you did."

"That was a nice thing to say," Isabelle replied.

"Well, guess what? Let me tell you how it made me feel. It made me feel ugly. It made me feel angry. Because I was feeling like I was still pretty on the outside as well. Just because I had put on weight, I didn't see myself as no longer pretty. Yes, I was bigger. Yes, I wasn't a size 5 anymore but I wanted to, needed to, feel that I was still attractive."

Isabelle stopped combing Emily's hair as she grabbed on to the back of her chair. She seemed to want to hug Emily, but she stopped herself. A tear started to fall down her right cheek.

"I didn't mean to hurt your feelings," Isabelle said. "I was trying to make you feel better. I figured you felt bad about the weight gain."

"I did feel bad about it, but I wanted those who care about me to see beyond the weight, beyond the pounds, to understand that something must have been going on inside me that I was driven to regain the weight. And to be patient with me, and to applaud my appearance, whether I lost the weight again or stayed obese."

"You were never obese!" Isabelle exclaimed.

"Yes, I was. Two hundred three pounds is obese. But I think I have a grip on it now. I think I can stay at this weight. I now have a better understanding about what was driving me to overeat."

Isabelle smiled and began combing Emily's hair again.

"So what can I do for you today? A trim?"

"No," Emily said. "Let's go for a new look. I really like the way Maria Shriver's hair falls on her face. Do you know who Maria Shriver is?"

"She's the wife of the governor of California," said Isabelle.

"She's also been a TV news announcer for one of the network prime time news shows and she just wrote an advice book for high school girls going off to college."

Emily picked up her dark brown designer pocketbook. She reached inside one of the zippered compartments and pulled out a photograph.

"Here," Emily said. "This is a picture of Maria Shriver. Do you think you could shape my hair the same way?"

"No problem," Isabelle said.

Emily smiled as she looked into the mirror. Staring back at her was a new Emily, a more relaxed Emily, and an Emily without secrets and demons. This Emily didn't have to keep eating to obliterate the good feelings that she felt when she was thin— feelings that scared her, feelings of unworthiness because of what she had endured as a child and teenager.

This Emily was proud, confident, and fearless.

As she stared in the mirror, she thought of her late therapist, Dr. Herbert Peters. She missed that man. He was so wise, so brilliant. She used to refer to him as her psychological guru. He was more than a therapist. He was like a sage from the East, all-wise, all-knowing. He was an interpreter of dreams, one of the highest callings someone could have. But he also had a problem letting go. Why hadn't he helped her to end her therapy before he died? Fourteen years. She might still be his patient if he had not died. And why hadn't he been honest about his illness?

Dr. Peters had taught Emily to stand up for herself and her life and to live in reality and not denial. But whenever Dr. Peters coughed and she asked him if he was okay, he'd reply, "I'm fine, just a little cold."

A little cold! He actually had terminal lung cancer, although she did not find that out until she got the call from Dr. Peters' girlfriend that he had died. And she thought of her late father.

"I'm dying," her father had said to her in the hospital about a week before he lost consciousness.

Maybe the delirium that he went into right before the end was nature's way of protecting her father from the psychic pain he must have been in once he accepted that he was dying.

She missed her father. And her brother.

As she thought of them, she found herself starting to feel hungry. But this time, she caught herself. She self-talked that the hunger was a response to the feelings she was having. It wasn't "real" hunger.

She was determined to remain this weight and to enjoy her renewed size 5 figure and the clothes that she bought to show it off. She was not going to go back up again, hiding her sensuality behind the fat and the weight and the inertia.

Emily looked in the mirror and remembered the time she went to the beauty parlor with her mother. She was in second grade and it was right before class picture day. Emily wanted a trim but her mother wanted her to get a permanent.

The permanent was so tight, including the little ringlets that were supposed to be bangs, that her buckteeth were even more accentuated. It was many years before braces would push her teeth back so she had an appealing smile. She was the laughing stock of her class. The class picture, with Emily wearing a checked pinafore, froze for all time the humiliation Emily felt about her appearance.

Too often she had felt that way throughout her life. She had done things to make herself feel and look that way. With her healing came an understanding of how her low self-esteem and self-confidence had allowed her to be abused. It also helped her give up the magical thinking that stopping the abuse had somehow caused her brother's death. That does not mean that each action—allowing herself to be abused rather than confiding in a caring adult who might have protected her as well as confessing the abuse and getting her brother to stop—did not have consequences. Each situation had immediate and long-term effects. But that is distinctly different from saying Emily was to blame for being victimized, or that refusing to continue being a victim made her responsible for her brother's death.

One of the mysterious and baffling parts of recovery that Emily had discovered through her long journey with Dr. Peters was that people have a need to repeat the trauma in their lives in an effort to overcome it. When Emily was in graduate school, they called it "repetition compulsion," the way someone was compelled to repeat the original trauma. But the term "repetition compulsion" sounded so clinical, and hopeless.

Dr. Peters' suggestion was that people need to repeat the trauma in order to have a different outcome—"because if you don't, you'll always be left with the problem." This helped to explain why so many of Emily's post-chain smoking efforts at losing, and keeping off, her surplus weight had failed. Understanding that basic fact about human nature helped her to see that by repeatedly gaining weight, she was turning herself into a victim again. In a society that rewards thinness and dressing well, Emily, till now, was uncomfortable in that role because, deep down inside, she felt she deserved to be fat and self-hating. It was necessary to heal her emotions before she could maintain her thinner, healthier, more attractive self.

Compulsive overeating also symbolized how out of control Emily felt about her life. The only thing she could control was what and when she put something in her mouth. Unless she took control of her overeating, she was victimizing herself; by becoming obese, she was punishing herself and preventing herself from enjoying her life, her body, and her sensuality.

But no more. She had finally become one of those beautiful, shapely, well-dressed, and successful women with a loving family and devoted friends that so many who did not have "it" loved to hate.

"That's their problem," Emily whispered under her breath as Isabelle trimmed her hair into the flattering style that she had chosen for herself.

GREG WOULD BE WAITING at home for Emily to return. They were going out to a movie and dinner. She'd go armed with her bottles of water, or buy water at the theater, and, yes, she was going to watch each and every thing she put into her mouth.

She knew how easily the "on" switch of compulsive overeating could take over her brain and lead her down the path of self-destruction yet again. This time, she was determined not to let that happen.

Yes, she knew all the statistics about how many who lose a lot of weight only regain the lost pounds, and then some. She had been one of those statistics! But that was then and this was now. The new, empowered Dr. Emily Taylor had awakened to the demons that she would have to face every waking moment. That was okay, though. This was even harder than giving up chain-smoking, or cutting up her credit cards after misusing them. Both addictions she was able to stop, cold turkey, and never do again.

But Emily now faced her demons at every meal, at every function. She would have to set the limits while still smelling the aroma of the food, tasting but not overindulging in chocolate or even the amount of protein she ate at any one meal.

It was a problem she would have to deal with for the rest of her life and she could either be on the winning or the losing side of the problem.

She decided that it felt a lot better to weigh less, enjoy her body, her sexuality, and to look to herself and people for fulfillment, not to food.

She also knew that she had to give up the perfectionism that was behind so much of her bingeing. That often translated into thinking that since she already fell off the wagon and didn't have a perfect day she might as well eat everything in sight. That attitude, as much as anything else, had sabotaged her weight control efforts.

"WOW," GREG SAID AS EMILY stepped out of the bathroom off the master bedroom wearing a new red negligee.

"You look amazing," he continued as she cuddled up to him on their king-sized bed. "You look good enough to eat," Greg said, pulling Emily down gently onto their bed.

"So what's stopping you?" she answered as they both softly laughed while Emily removed her red lace panties.

SHE HOPED THAT THE lifelong intermittent food bingeing and self-hate that began when she was a lonely, scared, and well-developed ten-year-old who did not know how to say "no" to her idolized older brother was finally over. She prayed that this time she had gotten deep enough into the cause of her overeating, bingeing, and food addiction that it was less likely she would relapse. Or, if she did relapse, that she would be able to stop it after five or, at the most, ten pounds, rather than having to ever again hit bottom, regaining almost all she had lost, to begin her long, arduous journey to a healthy figure yet again. Only time would tell if this was the last "big" weight loss she ever had to experience.

At least she felt more in control of her emotions and able to make other choices than compulsively overeating or bingeing whenever she got upset. Being upset, disappointed, angry, sad, and annoyed would occur no matter how happy, self-assured, satisfied, and at peace Emily might be with herself. At least now she was secure about her ability to cope when adversity challenged her. She committed herself to the wonderful notion that there were other, better ways to handle both adversity and the excessive energy that Emily realized she needed to harness for positive reasons as she had often done throughout her life.

IT WAS PERFECT TIMING when she got the call from her friend Kathleen. She and Greg had finished their lovemaking; they had even taken a short nap together.

"Can you meet me for coffee?" Kathleen asked.

"Sure. I'll be right there."

She and Kathleen had a favorite coffee shop about five minutes from Emily's house where they liked to meet. As long as Emily knew Kathleen—thirty-plus years—her friend preferred meeting at a coffee shop to an apartment or a house.

Kathleen had been away for several months for business and personal reasons.

TEN MINUTES LATER, EMILY arrived at the coffee shop. She searched the faces of everyone sitting at the tables or in over-stuffed arm chairs, as well as those waiting in line for their coffees and cups of tea.

Kathleen had been consistently thin for almost as long as they had been friends. Maybe once she gained ten extra pounds, but no one would consider Kathleen anything but a thin person without any kind of weight problem. Over the years, if Emily turned to food when she was nervous or upset, Kathleen instead would avoid eating.

Suddenly Emily caught site of a woman who looked vaguely familiar. But she was more than just plump. She was fat and puffy. Emily tried to compose herself and to avoid doing a double-take when she realized this woman was her friend Kathleen.

"Hello skinny," Kathleen said, hugging her friend.

"Great to see you," Emily replied, trying very hard to conceal her shock at Kathleen's size. She had gained thirty maybe even forty or more pounds in the couple of months since they had seen each other. Her face was bloated and her neck and arms were thick; her fingers and even her calves and feet were swollen.

If such a dramatic weight gain in a relatively short period of time could happen to Kathleen, it could happen to anyone, Emily thought.

"I'll be right back," Emily said. "I want to get some coffee."

She returned several minutes later, coffee cup in one hand and a low-fat muffin in another.

"You're eating a muffin?" Kathleen asked.

"Yes, why not?"

"Because you never used to let yourself eat muffins."

"At least not in front of you," Emily added, quickly. "But now, I've learned that I can eat a muffin, in moderation, and it's okay."

Switching the subject from food, Emily continued, "It's great to see you. Your e-mails have helped keep me in the loop but tell me more about what you've been up to since you left for Geneva."

"I realized my mother's death hit me harder than I thought," Kathleen began. "You know grief can actually change you physically."

For the next hour, Emily's old friend shared about her life and her grief with honesty and sharpness. But not one word was ever uttered by Kathleen or Emily about the weight gain and its sensational change in Kathleen's appearance. Emily knew her old friend would have brought it up if she wanted to discuss it.

EMILY RETURNED HOME FROM HER visit with Kathleen still amazed at the change in her friend's appearance but determined not to feel guilty that she was doing better with her own weight challenges. She fought that strong impulse and the pull backward to her old habit of bingeing. She was hungry so she took a bagel out of the bread basket, as well as some low-fat cream cheese, and she smeared it on half of the bagel. Then she frantically looked through all the various jars stored on the door of the refrigerator till she found her favorite preserves, raspberry. Next she measured exactly one teaspoon of raspberry preserves which she then spread all over half of the bagel.

Emily tasted the bagel and enjoyed each and every bite. She could have eaten the other half of the bagel, but she was full. Half of the bagel was enough.

Emily had just had something to eat when she was upset and hungry. But she knew that she was going to continue to also find other ways to deal with her rage, her anger, her nervousness, her self-doubt, when such feelings reemerged.

ALREADY SHE WAS MORE productive than she had been in years. Yes, she would have to always be concerned with what she ate. Like the diabetic who had to take insulin or someone with an underactive thyroid who had to take a medication for that condition, she would probably have to always weigh and measure what she ate (or at least be conscious about the portions of her food). That was just a fact of her life that she needed to accept so she could remain in control of her weight problem.

Emily shut down her computer and went into the bathroom outside her lower level office. She looked in the mirror at her bangs. She was letting her bangs grow out since she decided she liked the way she looked without bangs, with her forehead showing. As she stared in the mirror, she picked up a hairbrush and brushed her bangs to the side, exposing the two-inch scar on her forehead that she got when she was two that she had been trying to hide most of her life. Emily smiled as she looked in the mirror and continued brushing her bangs to the side. She no longer felt the need to cover up her scar. Not anymore. No reason at all.

About
The Author

JAN YAGER has a doctorate in sociology from The City University of New York where she was a National Science Foundation pre-doctoral fellow in medical sociology. She also has an MA in criminal justice from Goddard College and she did graduate work in art therapy at Hahnemann Medical College.

The former Janet (J.L.) Barkas, Jan Yager is the award-winning author of numerous nonfiction and fiction titles translated into 24 languages including *Victims, Friendshifts®: The Power of Friendship and How It Shapes Our Lives, When Friendship Hurts, Road Signs on Life's Journey, Work Less, Do More, Creative Time Management for the New Millennium, 365 Daily Affirmations for Creative Weight Management,* and, with her husband Fred Yager, of two suspense novels: *Just Your Everyday People* and *Untimely Death.*

The author has taught criminology and sociology courses at Temple University, St. John's University, and the University of Connecticut, among other colleges. For more than a decade, Jan Yager has been conducting original research on eating disorders and being the survivor of childhood or teenage sexual abuse.

Interviewed often by print and broadcast media including *The Oprah Winfrey Show, The Today Show, The Early Show, Good Morning America, The View, Nightline, Sunday Morning,* BBC radio, the *New York Times,* the *Wall Street Journal,* and *USA Today,* Jan is a professional speaker, coach, and consultant.

Jan and her husband Fred reside in Fairfield County, Connecticut. They are parents of two grown sons and a grandson.

For more information about the author, go to:

www.janyager.com or www.fredandjanyager.com.

www.ingramcontent.com/pod-product-compliance
Lightning Source LLC
Chambersburg PA
CBHW030524020726
47494CB00004B/1223